SLAY RIDE

OLIVIA DUNKLEY

© **Copyright 2025 - All rights reserved.**

The content within this book may not be reproduced, duplicated or transmitted without direct written permission from the author or the publisher.

Under no circumstances will any blame or legal responsibility be held against the publisher, or author, for any damages, reparation, or monetary loss due to the information contained within this book. Either directly or indirectly. You are responsible for your own choices, actions, and results.

Legal Notice:

This book is copyright protected. This book is only for personal use. You cannot amend, distribute, sell, use, quote or paraphrase any part, of the content within this book, without the consent of the author or publisher.

Disclaimer Notice:

Please note the information contained within this document is for educational and entertainment purposes only. All effort has been expended to present accurate, up-to-date, and reliable, complete information. No warranties of any kind are declared or implied. Readers acknowledge that the author is not engaging in the rendering of legal, financial, medical or professional advice. The content within this book has been derived from various sources. Please consult a licensed professional before attempting any techniques outlined in this book.

By reading this document, the reader agrees that under no circumstances is the author responsible for any losses, direct or indirect, which are incurred as a result of the use of the information contained within this document, including, but not limited to, — errors, omissions, or inaccuracies.

CONTENTS

Prologue	5
1. Detective Donner	19
2. Kris	24
3. Holly	28
4. Holly	35
5. Kris	42
6. Holly	46
7. Holly	53
8. Detective Donner	64
9. Kris	69
10. Holly	74
11. Holly	83
12. Holly	92
13. Detective Donnor	98
14. Holly	105
15. Kris	109
16. Holly	113
17. Kris	124
18. Holly	126
19. Holly	144
20. Kris	151
21. Holly	154
22. Kris	160
23. Holly	163
24. Kris	165
25. Holly	168
26. Detective Donner	172
27. Holly	176
28. Kris	183
29. Holly	185
30. Kris	188
31. Detective Donner	193

32. Holly	197
33. Detective Donner	200
34. Holly	208
Epilogue	215

PROLOGUE

Pine needles tickle my face as I scoot a little closer to the presents underneath the Christmas tree. I hope the big red box is mine. It's the biggest one under the Christmas tree, and the prettiest too. Mom knows red is my favourite colour and bigger is always better when it comes to presents.

I look at the other presents under the tree. They are all wrapped in white paper with little silver snowflakes. They look a little boring, and none of them is big enough to be the bike I asked Santa for in my letter. I bite my lip as I wonder again if Santa got my letter. Mom says Santa's elves help him read all the letters from little boys and girls, and that they would never lose one, but I still worry. I hope Santa got mine in time. I really want that bike.

I glance down at the crayons in my hand, then back at the white boxes. *Maybe I can draw something on them to make them more colourful.* I scoot a little closer, then hesitate. Mom might get mad. She always says how good my drawings are, but she also told me not to touch the presents under the tree. I look down at my crayons again. Maybe just one drawing for Santa. I pick one of the presents and start to draw a picture of Santa on it. *What if he sees it and thinks I'm a really good artist and takes me to the North Pole to help the elves!?* I lean forward, avoiding the sharp pine needles of our Christmas tree, and begin coloring in Santa's suit.

"Kris," Dad calls from behind me. I stop and look at him over my shoulder, pretending I wasn't doing anything at all.

"Yeah, Dad?" I smile.

Dad's face pulls into a grimace. He looks at me with a dark, stern expression, and my tummy starts to get that sort of sick feeling it gets when Dad is mad. He looks funny tonight. His hair is messy, and his shirt has wrinkles in it. He would never let me wear a shirt with wrinkles in it like that.

Dad takes a sip from the brown bottle he is holding and looks out the window. I never know what's going to happen when he drinks what's in the brown bottles. Sometimes he gets nicer; he'll laugh and hug Mom and let me stay up late, but other times he gets mad... scary. I silently hope today is a laughing day; after all, it is Christmas Eve, and Santa is coming.

"Are you trying to get your gift?" Dad asks me. But before I can answer, he says, "I'm watching you." He says it in a sort of eerie, sing-song voice, and I think it means that it's a laughing day.

I cup my hands around my mouth and whisper to him. "I'm drawing Santa a picture on this one!"

Dad is staring at me, but I don't think he sees me. His eyes suddenly shift to the window.

I'm not sure if Dad is mad that I'm drawing on the presents or not. I try to recapture his attention. "It's okay, Dad? Mom won't be mad?" I ask, looking back at my drawing on the box. It looks weird, unfinished, and I want to start coloring again, but I wait for Dad to answer.

"Who cares?" Dad scoffs.

My brow crinkles in confusion, but I decide he means it's okay. I finish coloring Santa's suit, then start adding a Christmas tree and some presents to the picture. As I reach for my crayons, the front door opens, and Mom walks in, a phone pressed to her ear, her hands gripping bags. Dad watches her, a weird expression on his face. He takes a big sip from the brown bottle, his jaw bulging.

Mom sets down the bags she is carrying and then says goodbye to whoever is on the phone. She hangs up and then sets her phone down.

"Hey, honey," Mom calls out, and I answer, "Hey, Mom". She walks around the couch to the Christmas tree and crouches down beside me. She smiles at me under the tree. "Is this my present?" She asks, ruffling my hair.

"Mom!" I say, swatting at her hand.

"Best present ever," she says.

I see Dad watching us, and I realize they aren't looking at or talking to each other. My tummy starts to get that sick feeling. I don't like it when they aren't talking. Mom stands up but still looks down at me. "You aren't thinking of opening any of those, right?"

"Nooo," I say, shaking my head from side to side as I make the word long.

Mom smiles. "Good." She puts her hands on her hips. "Why don't I start some dinner?"

I turn back to the presents. I need to get to work if I want to finish before bedtime. Taking the blue crayon, I pick up one of the white presents. I think I'll draw a happy face for Dad so he'll always be happy. I begin to scribble on the package in my lap. I smile. It looks way better with some color on it.

"Where have you been?" I hear Dad ask. "It's Christmas Eve."

"I went to Sarah's. She needed help with some last-minute presents. She hasn't quite been herself ever since Dave left."

"Do I look like I fucking care about Sarah?" Dad asks. "Your place is here, taking care of your family."

I turn and look at my dad. It's not going to be a laughing night. It's going to be the other kind... the scary kind.

"You're drinking," Mom says, and even I can hear the disappointment and- *what's the opposite of surprise?*-Resignation in her voice. "Did you really think that was a good idea? It's Christmas Eve."

I shrink into myself. Soon, the shouting will start.

"Yes. It is Christmas Eve." Dad says, rising up off the couch so he's standing. Mom looks small next to him. "And while Santa Claus is handing out presents to good boys and girls, what we really need is someone to punish the naughty."

He grabs Mom by the arm and jerks her towards him. She pulls back, yanking her arm out of his grasp.

"Get your hands off me." She says.

I can hear the fear in her voice. Dad must have had more bottles than I realized if he's already ready to hurt us.

"Did you think I wouldn't find out? You lying little slut?" Dad grabs Mom again, and she pushes and struggles at the hand holding her, but she can't break free.

I crawl behind the Christmas tree and make sure not to cry. Dad hates it when I cry.

"What are you talking about?" She yells, pushing furiously at Dad. "Nicholas?" Mom's voice is desperate.

Dad starts to sing. "He knows where you are sleeping. He sees that you're awake. He knows that you've been bad, not good. Shoulda been good for your life's sake."

"Nicholas, stop it." She pushes at him again, and he seems to relax his hold on her, though he doesn't let go. He leans into her and looks her in the eye. "You've been naughty." He says.

Mom's brow wrinkles in confusion, and she gives him a look. "I've been naughty? Would you like to explain how?"

Dad takes another long, slow drink from his bottle, holding onto Mom's wrist all the while so she can't escape.

"I know you weren't with Sarah," He says, his voice almost amused. His voice softens, almost to a whisper, as he leans in closer to Mom. "And I was just sitting here wondering where you got the damn balls to cheat on me." Suddenly, he reaches out and grabs Mom by the neck. His huge hand wraps almost entirely around it. Mom tries to pull away, gasping and struggling, but Dad picks her up and pulls her closer using only that one hand around her neck. "Me! Do you know how many women would love to be with me? Do you know how lucky you are that I chose you?" Dad chuckles. "And this is how you repay me?"

I can't take my eyes off my mom. Her face is turning the color of one of my crayons... Purple? She's choking and gasping. Mom is wide-eyed, tears streaming down her face. Dad's face is red with anger, but he's laughing.

"Dad, stop!" I yell. Running up to them. I pull on Dad's arm, but he doesn't notice me. "Dad!" I say, my voice high and squeaky.

Suddenly, he drops her. Mom collapses to the floor, breathing heavily. Her face goes from purple to red. But dad isn't done. He reaches down and grabs a handful of her hair. Mom cries out in pain.

Dad leans down. He's sweating. He twists the hair in his hand, and Mom cries out again.

I hit dad with my fist in the back. "Stop it! Stop it!"

Dad doesn't even look at me, just reaches back and pushes me.

I fly across the room and hit the floor, my head smacking against the polished wood.

Mom screams and tries to get free to come to me. "Don't you touch him," she shrieks. But no matter how hard she struggles, she can't get away from that grip he has on her hair.

Dad just smiles. "Lying and cheating." He shakes his head and tsk's. "And during Christmas no less. Shame on you. What would Santa say? He'll have to put you on the naughty list."

"Nicholas," Mom begs. "I swear to you, I haven't cheated. There is no one else. I love you. Only you!" But she sounds like she isn't telling the truth, and we're always supposed to tell the truth.

I'm still lying on my back in the same position as when I hit the floor after Dad pushed me. I look at Mom. Tears pour down her cheeks. She is holding onto Dad's hand in her hair with both hands.

Dad suddenly lets go of Mom, and she collapses to the floor. Dad picks up the brown bottle and takes a drink.

Mom starts crawling across the floor towards me. She reaches me and pulls me into her arms. "It's okay, honey." She coos. "Everything is gonna be okay. Are you hurt?' She asks and brushes the hair out of my eyes. She smiles lovingly at me. I'm about to tell her I'm okay, but I see Dad come up behind her, dark and scary. I open my mouth to warn her, but I'm too late. She is yanked away from me. She screams in pain as he pulls her up.

"Go ahead, Mary. Lie to me again. Tell me you aren't fucking another man. Giving him what's rightfully mine."

Mom whimpers. "I promise you... I'm not..."

Dad turns and violently throws his bottle against the wall. It crashes into pieces. I look at mom. She's gonna be mad. Now she'll have to clean up that mess. But Mom only looks frightened.

"Lie to me again, and I'll kill you!" Dad screams.

I pull my knees to my chest and cover my ears. I feel something cold slide down my cheeks. I start to cry in earnest, big heaving sobs.

Mom turns to look at me. Her face is filled with compassion and... what I would later learn is resignation. She turns to Dad.

"Okay. Yes, Nicholas, I'm fucking another man. One who treats me with compassion and respect. One who likes who I am and is nice to me. He's ten times the man you are, and I'm not just sleeping with him, I love him, and he loves me."

Dad suddenly looks thoughtful. He bends down and picks up a piece of glass, turning it around in his hands as if he were studying it. He moves towards mom, but she steps back, putting the couch between them. Dad starts to sing.

"On the first day of Christmas, my true love murdered me," Dad sings as he slowly strides toward her, like a predator. "By hanging me from a tree."

Mom moves away from him, keeping the couch between them. She's scared. I'm scared too. Suddenly, she dashes for the door, and for a moment I think she's gonna leave me, but she doesn't leave. She grabs her purse, reaches inside, and pulls out a gun. For a moment, I think it's my toy gun from upstairs, but Dad suddenly stops moving.

"What are you going to do, Mary? Shoot me?" He laughs, then. A big belly laugh. "My, my, you have been naughty!"

"I don't want to shoot you, Nicholas. Just let Kristofer and me go. Let us leave, and it will all be over."

Dad keeps strolling towards her. Mom's hand shakes. "Please, Nicholas. Don't make me do this." But Dad doesn't stop.

"Do you really think I would let you leave me? And take my son?" Dad's voice is calm and even, as he stalks closer and closer to Mom. Tears are streaming down her cheeks, but her voice is even when she says, "You're going to have to." Suddenly, she pulls the trigger. A loud BANG hurts my ears, and I jump. I cover my ears and close my eyes.

But the next moment, I hear mom shriek. My eyes fly open, and I see Dad lunge at her. *Didn't she shoot him?* She must have missed, and now dad is pushing her up against the front door. I climb up onto the couch so I can see. Mom and Dad are wrestling over the gun. Mom is sweating, her face red, and she is making a loud shrieking sound as Dad, who seems somewhat relaxed, forces the gun out of her hand.

Mom releases it with a final sob. She sags.

Dad takes the gun and throws it carelessly onto the couch. I stare at it. It almost hit me when Dad threw it. Mom sees my expression, and she suddenly pushes forward against my dad.

"Kris, pick it up!" Mom commands. "Get the gun. Get the gun, sweetheart." She struggles against my dad, then suddenly knees him between the legs. Dad grunts loudly and lets her go.

Mom is already running towards me. "The gun, Kris. Get the gun. Give it to me." But I feel frozen. I can't make my body move. I look down at the gun sitting so conveniently at my feet. But I can't make myself reach down and grasp it.

Mom is almost to me when she is suddenly pulled up short. Dad has her from behind. She struggles, pushing against him.

"Kris! The gun! Hand it to me!" She screams, then turns and scratches Dad across the face. Dad lets go of her with a grunt of pain, but then balls his hand into a fist and swings it into Mom's face. I hear a crunching noise, and Mom suddenly collapses.

"Mom!" I scream. Dad looks at me, breathing heavily. He's got blood dripping down his side. I guess Mom did hit him after all.

"Good boy," Dad says. He cups my face with one of his hands, but it's covered in blood, and he leaves the wet sticky substance on my face. I cringe.

Dad picks Mom up off the floor. She is mumbling something, but I can't understand it. She looks up at me, and my mouth flies open in shock. Her face is black and blue, cut open and bleeding. I reach for her, but Dad drags her away from me.

"Let's sit down, shall we?" Dad says. He sits Mom on the couch. She falls over. She can't sit up. Dad sits on the couch next to her.

"Would you like to open one of your presents?" Dad asks me. I look at my dad, but I can't make sense of his words.

"Shouldn't we help Mom?" I ask. "She's bleeding."

"Mom's been bad, Kris. And do you know what happens to naughty girls on Christmas?"

I nod, "They get coal in their stocking."

"Not this year. This year, Santa is punishing the naughty. It's past time, don't you think?" Dad says almost jovially. "Why don't you open one of your Christmas presents?" He says to me again. He looks at Mom, slumped over on the couch, her eyes dazed and unseeing. "You'd like that. Wouldn't you, dear?"

I want to go to my mom and let her hold me. Whenever Dad gets like this, she always comes to my room and holds me afterward. I glance towards the gun. I think about getting it and pointing it at my dad. Dad follows my gaze, and a look comes over his face. "Kris, don't make me put you on the naughty list." He says as he leans forward and pushes me towards the tree. I stumble and then fall to my knees.

"Go ahead," Dad says. "Pick a present."

I watch as he picks up Mom, smiling maniacally. He pulls her against him and rubs his nose over her cheeks and down her neck. Mom's eyes close, and she starts to cry. I want to help, but I can't move.

"Well, open it!" Dad commands. I look down and realize I'm holding a present. The red one. I open it and pull out the toy inside. It's the six-piece dinosaur set I told Mom I wanted. Suddenly, I feel like throwing up.

Dad laughs jovially. "Merry Christmas! Merry Christmas!"

Mom slumps off the couch and starts crawling on her hands and knees towards me. "Thank you, Mama," I say, holding up the dinosaur set I know she's gotten me for Christmas.

She reaches a hand towards me, but it shakes violently. I reach out and almost take it, when suddenly Dad smacks her hand away.

"Didn't you hear me, Kris?" He roars in my face, and I cringe inwardly but don't cower away from him. He hates it when I move away from him. "Your mom is bad. She's been sleeping with another man. That's bad." He enunciates the words as he screams them right into my face.

"Stop it. Stop it." Mom's words come out as little more than a whisper.

"And this is what naughty girls get for Christmas." My dad says almost casually, as he reaches down and grabs Mom's hair. He pulls her head up, and she lets out a small moan. Then, Dad reaches down and cuts Mom's throat.

I stare at my mom. It happened so quickly that both of us were caught off guard. I stare at the blood pouring down Mom's neck as her eyes bulge in horror at the sudden realization of what's happened.

"No! Mommy!" I whisper. Blood pours down her neck and onto her blouse. There's so much blood. She gurgles and falls to her side. Dad starts to laugh, but I can't take my eyes off my mom. She turns and looks at me, blood pouring out of her mouth and down her neck. She pulls herself towards me, crawling across the floor.

She tries to speak. "It's alright..." But blood spurts out of her mouth, and it lands on my arm. The blood. I want it off me! I push back away from her and the blood pooling on the floor.

Mom shudders, and her arms give out. She lies on the carpet, as the blood seeps out of her, making a big red circle around her head. I can smell the metal scent mixing with her perfume.

Dad laughs, "See, Mary? You should have been good! Right, Kris? Tell mommy she should have been good!"

Mom lies still on the floor, her eyes open, but she doesn't see me, and she doesn't blink. Her eyes are blank and vacant. "Mom?" I feel tears in my eyes, and I hurriedly wipe them away. Dad hates it when I cry.

Mom just lies there. I can't look away from her, and I don't move closer because I don't want to get the blood on my pants and shirt. Mom wouldn't like that. Dad is laughing now. Laughing and laughing. "I'm mother fucking Santa Claus." He announces jovially and then starts singing about not crying because Santa is coming to town.

Dad goes to the kitchen for another brown bottle, and I lean towards my mom. "Mommy?" I whisper. "Mommy?" I feel scared, and sad, and a little crazy.

Suddenly, I hear sirens. Yes! I think. They came to help my mom! Dad frowns at the noise outside, but I feel relieved. They are going to help my mom. The front door bursts open, and Dad yells at the men who come in. "Hey, you can't just barge in here. This is private property."

But the men with black uniforms and guns see mom and all the blood and start shouting at dad to put his hands behind his back. They push him down before I can blink. "Dad!" I yell out. I have a horrible feeling in the pit of my stomach. No! Not dad too! Please! I need someone to take care of me!

Dad's hands are being handcuffed behind his back. I start to cry. Dad tries to fight off the men and come to me, but the men grab him and pull him back. Dad ends up on his knees, unable to stand with his hands behind his back. The police officers pull Dad to his feet and start to haul him towards the open door. He calls to me as they do. "This was your mom's fault, Kris. She was bad! Naughty! Do you understand? I had to put her on the naughty list. Do you hear me, Kris? Let go of me! Merry Christmas, Kris!"

1

DETECTIVE DONNER
THIRTY-TWO YEARS LATER

The rain congeals on my windshield, making the world outside curvy and unclear like an image in a funhouse mirror. I flick the wipers up another notch, watching the droplets scatter. The radio crackles with dispatch updates, but I'm not listening. My hands tighten on the wheel.

Victim number eleven.

She's waiting for me in a two-story colonial on Maple Drive, just like the others. A nice house. A quiet street. The kind of place where people leave their doors unlocked and wave to their neighbors. Or at least, they used to. I pull up behind the coroner's van, my headlights cutting through the downpour that will soon turn into a blizzard. It's been unseasonably warm, but it's getting late, and the temperature is already dropping.

The front door is open, uniformed officers moving in and out like shadows. I don't rush. I already know what's inside—another doll. I grip the steering wheel tight enough that my knuckles go white. *How can this be happening?* I wonder for the thousandth time. *How can we know who is committing these atroc-*

ities, have had him under our control for the last 7 years, and still have no idea where he is, how he's finding his victims, or how to catch him?

How had they let him escape in the first place? This thought has plagued me. It's not like we didn't know what he was capable of.

But, at least, I don't have to add the weight of that responsibility to the guilt eating at my gut. The asylum isn't my department. Still... He was so easy to catch the first time. This time, he's like a ghost.

And now another girl is dead because I'm not smart enough or fast enough or working hard enough or just not *enough*. If I were, I would have caught this guy after the fifth, or eighth, or even tenth victim.

I take a deep breath and exit my shop. The very least I can do is go look the girl in the face and tell her I'm sorry. Of course, I do that part in my head so my officers don't think I've gone completely insane.

The first thing that hits me is the smell—coppery blood, cloying perfume, and underneath it all, the faint, nauseating sweetness of decay. The living room is dim, the only light coming from a single lamp knocked onto its side, casting long, jagged shadows. And there, beneath the bay window, next to the Christmas tree in an old, oak rocking chair, is the girl. *God help me.*

She's propped up like a child's toy, legs stiffly together, hands folded in her lap. Her throat is slit ear to ear, the wound so precise it could've been done with a scalpel. But it's the rest of it that makes my stomach twist.

Her cheeks are rouged with bright pink circles that have been painted on post mortem. Her lips are smeared red, the lines imperfect, as if she's been playing with her mother's makeup. Fake lashes are drawn over her closed eyelids in thick, uneven strokes. And the clothes—God, the clothes. A frilly white dress, short lace socks, black patent-leather shoes that gleam under the flickering light.

A doll. That's what he turns them into. Dolls under the Christmas tree. As if they're a gift for those who find them.

I crouch beside her, gloved hands hovering over the scene without touching. The dress is new. The last victim wore something similar—pink gingham, like something out of a 1950s catalog. Before that, it was a blue pinafore, then a yellow sundress. Always childlike. Always pristine.

Where the hell is he getting the dresses?

I push myself up, my knees protesting. The room spins for a second, and I steady myself against the wall. Too much coffee. Not enough sleep. No one is surprised at finding her. There have been 10 victims before her. One each day for the last 10 days. Each one with the same MO. We knew if we didn't catch him in time, that there would be another one, and here she is.

I'm so sorry. I silently apologize to the dead woman sitting under her Christmas tree.

His victims are so random, always women, but they couldn't be more different. They are from all different classes and parts of the city, with every hair color and eye color. *Of course, they all have the same vice.*

"Detective?" Officer Cane interrupts my thoughts. He steps into the doorway, his face pale. "You should see the bedroom."

I follow him down the hall, my shoes sticking slightly to the hardwood. The bedroom door is ajar, and when I push it open, the smell hits me again—stronger this time.

The bedroom is a mess; the bed rumpled, with a massive blood stain darkening the carpet. This is obviously where he killed her. He likes to find them in bed. It fits with his adopted persona, Santa Claus.

Cane exhales sharply beside me. "Number eleven. Eleven victims in eleven days."

"Yeah," I mutter. "And if we don't catch him, there's gonna be another one tomorrow on Christmas Eve."

Cane shakes his head, "I can't believe we can't catch this guy. I feel like he's trying to make it so easy."

I look at Cane, confused, "What do you mean?"

"The twelve days of Christmas," he answers. "Twelve victims for the twelve days of Christmas. He's made it so obvious that he is here. That he's going to kill again. It's almost like he's toying with us." Cane looks thoughtful, and an unhappy expression steals over his features. "I can't believe we can't catch him," He says again.

"Yeah," I say tiredly. *I should've retired last year.*

Thirty years on the force, twenty-two in homicide, and nothing —nothing—has ever crawled under my skin like this. Not the drug wars in the nineties. Not the serial arsonist who lit up half the industrial district. This? This is something else.

This is personal.

I'd known the first victim.

Emily Shaw. She'd only been twenty-four. She'd worked at the diner on Fifth. She used to bring me coffee every morning, black, no sugar, before the end of her shift. I'd found her beneath her own Christmas tree, dressed in a plaid jumper, her hair braided like a schoolgirl's.

That was December 13th. Ten bodies later, and the FBI still hasn't sent anyone to take over this shit show. "After the holidays," they'd said, like these girls didn't matter, like this psycho gave a damn about office hours.

I step back into the hallway, pulling out my phone. No new calls. No new leads. Just another dead girl and a killer who's laughing at us. Cane lingers in the doorway. "We've got to figure out who he's targeting next."

I don't answer because there is nothing to say. We have zero leads, no idea how he's picking his victims, *how he knows... How the hell does he know?*

I've asked myself this question a hundred times. If only we could put out a public statement. "If you're cheating on your husband, you're a target." But most of them still wouldn't take the proper precautions. Hell, I'm not even sure what precautions they should be taking. It seems like this guy is waltzing into these women's houses, murdering them, then playing dress up, all without breaking a sweat. I run a hand down my face.

Okay. Breaks over. Time to go in and find something... *anything* that will help break this case.

I turn around and head back to the dead woman in the chair.

"Please," I silently beg, *"give me something, or someone else is going to die."*

2

KRIS

Rain slips down the bridge of my nose, tickling my lips in an almost soothing way. I lick the water off my lips, then try to brush my wet hair out of my eyes. It sticks to my face. I try again and then slap it away with both hands repeatedly in frustration when it still won't move. Finally, I'm free of it.

Concerned, I glance across the street to see if I've been noticed, but the officers are still shuffling in and out of the house, their expressions forlorn. *They look like someone died.* I laugh at the thought. *Like someone died!* I giggle again, unable to help myself.

They found my doll. She'd been so beautiful. I smile to myself, thinking of the careful way I had fixed her hair and face, pleased remembering how she'd looked there beneath the Christmas tree. I hope these officers appreciated the effort I'd put into making it a nice surprise.

I frown at the drawn looks on the officer's faces. *Why do they look so unhappy?* Didn't they know she was naughty? *Naughty!* And it was my job to punish the naughty. Shouldn't these men understand that more than anyone? We have the same job! ...

Only I make it nice. I take a lot of time making it nice for everyone. As Santa Claus, I guess it's part of the job, but still, a little appreciation would be nice. These officers don't seem to appreciate my work. "They're naughty," I mutter. "They're all naughty."

I think back on this last punishment. It had been one of the easier ones. She hadn't screamed much, just cried... like Mother.

I flex my fingers against the rough fabric of my pants, still sticky under my gloves. The blood always gets everywhere, no matter how careful I am. I can still smell it. I resist the urge to bring my fingers to my nose and breathe deeply. Mom would hate the mess.

For a moment, I allow myself to enjoy the memory of the wet, sticky substance seeping through my fingers. Unable to resist, I bring my fingers to my face and take a long inhale through my nose. The smell soothes me. It reminds me of Mom. A memory flickers—Mother on the living room floor, her blood fanning around her like spilled wine, Dad standing over her, the Christmas tree lights reflected in his wide, crazy eyes. "You see, Kris? It's what naughty girls get for Christmas."

That was the night I'd found out that Dad was Santa Claus, but then the officers had taken him away.

I frown again at the officers across the street. I recognize some of them. Some of them had been there all those years ago. They'd come again to take me to the asylum after the first time I'd punished someone. That time had been harder. I hadn't wanted to do it—the blood. I hated the mess. But Dad wouldn't leave me alone. "Someone has to punish the naughty." He kept saying, over and over. "Don't make me put you on the naughty list." I suddenly shudder just thinking about what would happen if Dad put me on the naughty list. Then I'd end up like Mom.

The detective finally arrives, and I click my tongue at him. *So slow. He's so slow. How will he ever catch me?* I liked the detective. He'd been one of the officers who had taken me away and locked me up. It had been nice. I'd stayed for a while. It had been better to be taken care of, listened to, restrained. But Dad wouldn't leave me alone. He was so mad, so disappointed that I wasn't doing my job. "They took me away, Kris. It's up to you."

"They took me away too, Dad," I would tell him, but that just made him mad.

"Don't be such a pussy, boy. Stop crying! Get out of this place, and do your job like a man."

Thinking about Dad's relentless voice makes me want to cry, but I don't. Dad hates it when I cry. *Dad isn't here*, a voice whispers in the back of my mind. But he'll be back. He always comes back. He never leaves me alone for long.

Dad had been right. It had been easy to leave. The orderlies hadn't even noticed when I'd slipped out of my restraints. The nurses' station had been empty. But then they'd probably been trying to stop the bleeding. "Ho, ho, ho!" I laugh to myself thinking about it. They always try to stop the bleeding…

The first punishment had been the hardest. The blood! My hands had shaken so badly I nearly dropped the knife. But Dad's voice had been there, whispering in my ear. The memory of him doing it to Mom replaying in my head, a lesson on how I should do it.

It had gotten easier with each one, and I was almost done. Tomorrow was Christmas Eve—one more.

The twelfth one…

The twelfth one was special.

Holly.

"On the twelfth day of Christmas, my true love murdered me..." I smile, tapping my fingers against the tree I'm hiding behind in time with the music.

She doesn't know it yet, but she's the naughtiest of them all. Pretending to be Mother. Pretending to be good.

But I know the truth.

And on the twelfth day of Christmas, she'll learn what happens to liars and cheats.

The detective, who only arrived a few minutes ago, is already leaving. The rain pours through the shine of his headlights, each drop visible in the band of light. He never turned them off.

He was one of the officers who took me to the asylum. He looks old and tired, like he hasn't slept in weeks. He pauses on the porch, his gaze sweeping the street.

"I'm right here," I sing softly to myself. I know he wants me—wants to stop me from finishing my work. But he can't. No one can stop Santa Claus.

For a second, I think he sees me, but I make myself invisible, and he turns away.

Of course he does.

Santa Claus is magic, and magic can't be caught.

3
HOLLY

The sharp tap of my heels against the cold asphalt echoes in the deserted Straw Market parking lot. I shiver as a chilly breeze rakes across my bare legs. My dress, perfect for the office party, now feels ridiculously short in the cold December air. However, it had shown off my legs beautifully, and I'd gotten more than one compliment for my trouble.

The sparkly red heels I'd worn with the dress are starting to make my feet ache, but they are extraordinary, and I feel sexy just wearing them. I pull my jacket tighter around my shoulders, then free my long blonde ponytail from my jacket collar as I round my black Lexus. I fish my phone out of my purse, my fingers tapping impatiently as I dial Barry's number. My breath clouds the air in front of me, temporarily blurring the screen.

The gas station looms ahead, a gaudy splash of light against the night. The bell above the door chimes as I push it open. The air inside is thick with the scent of artificial pine and stale coffee. The place is nearly empty. The TV is playing, and the cashier doesn't bother to look away from the screen to see who's just walked in.

The phone rings one more time before Barry answers. "Have you left yet?" He asks without saying hello. His voice is strained and frustrated. I start down the aisle of chips, my eyes skimming the brightly coloured bags. *Doritos or Ruffles?*

"Yes," I say, as I grab a Diet Coke from the cooler. Condensation beads on the can, cold and wet against my palm.

"Oh. Were you the first one to leave?" Surprise, then a hint of something else... W*orry?* Sounds in his words. I grab a few things off the shelf.

"No. Lucy disappeared without telling anyone," I say, skimming over the candy options. *Do I need more candy for stockings?*

"Smart. Why didn't we think of that?" He chuckles.

"Right?!" I answer. "It was hilarious. Jeff wanted to run some numbers by her at the party, but couldn't find her. When he finally called her, she was already on the freeway. I snuck out while he was complaining that she'd left before the secret Santa exchange." I press the phone awkwardly between my shoulder and my cheek, a display of nuts in festive tins catching my eye. I grab a small bag of cashews, a sudden, inexplicable craving for salt hitting me.

"So, you also left before the secret Santa exchange?" Barry asks, sounding amused.

"Yes, but in my defense, I forgot to buy anything." I shrug. *Who needs a secret Santa gift from a stranger anyway?*

"Serves them right for having the company party on Christmas Eve!" My husband says. "Are you almost here?"

"Yeah, I just stopped at the Straw Market to get a couple of things." I glance at my watch, a sharp pang of guilt twisting in my stomach. I can hear Beau's excited little voice muffled through the phone, along with the distinct sound of presents being shaken.

"Okay, well, hurry... Beau is waiting for you." He tries to keep the accusation out of his voice, but isn't entirely successful. Barry's mad I chose the company Christmas party over being home with our son on Christmas Eve. Guilt cloys at me for a split second before it's gone. I probably should have stayed home, but my job is important to me, and I'll still be home in time to celebrate.

"How sweet," I say, trying to keep the defensiveness out of my voice.

"Uh, yeah..." Barry hesitates, "I kinda told him he could open a present tonight, and now he can hardly contain himself."

I suddenly understand the hesitation in my husband's voice. "Why would you tell him that?" I ask, sharply.

"Because it's Christmas Eve and his mother isn't here." This time, he doesn't bother holding back. His voice is full of accusation.

"Nice, Barry. You know I had no choice. What was I supposed to do? Miss the annual company Christmas party?" I feel both guilty and angry. *It wasn't my fault they planned the party on Christmas Eve.*

"I was just trying to make it a memorable Christmas and get him excited," Barry says. "It's one present. What's the big deal?"

I try not to see red, reminding myself that it's Christmas Eve and our son deserves to celebrate without his parents fighting for once, but I lose the inner battle.

"Well, it was *me* who actually went out, bought presents for our son, wrapped them, and put them under the tree," I hiss, setting all my things on the checkout counter. "I've worked really hard to make sure he has a nice Christmas. So, it seems a little unfair, after you've done practically nothing..."

"Except help pay for them..." Barry mutters.

"Exactly! And now, you've told him he can open one, you don't even know what they are." My voice has gotten overly loud for the quiet store, but it's hard for me to care.

"Jeez, Holly, he seemed unhappy that you weren't here, so I told him that when you got home, we'd open one of his presents."

Barry grows increasingly annoyed, but I roll my eyes at his tone. "If Beau was unhappy, all you had to do was put on the Grinch, or Scrooged, or read him a story." I glance at the cashier, a little embarrassed to be having this fight with him listening, but he isn't paying me any mind. His eyes are glued to the television. A soft murmur comes from its speaker, but it's too low for me to understand. I turn to the TV. *What could have him so enthralled?* I roll my eyes. It's the news.

"Fine. Okay? I'm sorry," Barry huffs. "But the damage is done, so, pretty please with a cherry on top, hurry home." He says sarcastically.

My husband is such a jerk.

"Fine." I over-enunciate. "Make sure he waits till I get there."

"Yeah." He hangs up.

I try not to let the fact that he hung up on me piss me off even more, and take a deep, calming breath. I promised myself no fighting over the holidays, but that is proving nearly impossible. How convenient for Barry that all these presents just show up wrapped under the Christmas tree, and then he's like, "Here, son, open a present," as if he had anything to do with them.

I force myself to stop thinking about it as I take several more deep breaths. Well, now Christmas Eve is ruined, at least for me.

I put my phone in my coat pocket, then look at the cashier behind the counter. Even with the scene I was just making, he is glued to the television screen. I turn to the TV, curious what could be holding his attention so. It's still the news. Doesn't he know that there is only bad news on the news? That they play on your fears to keep you watching.

True to form, a reporter stands in front of yellow police tape, her voice somber. *"...is yet another victim of the Kris Kringle Killer. Making this the eleventh victim in as many days..."* The flashing blue and red lights of police cruisers reflect in the glass of the refrigerators behind me. *"...There is conjecture that the killer, in a grotesque distortion of the holiday, has aligned these murders with the twelve days of Christmas, which means he isn't done yet."*

"Hello?" I wave a hand at the cashier, finally snapping him out of his trance. He rings me up slowly, brows furrowed like he's deep in thought.

"...Police recommend that you don't walk the city streets alone..." the reporter continues.

"That'll be $13.37," the cashier mumbles.

I pull out a twenty-dollar bill and hand it to him. The reporter is now interviewing a police officer. The cashier hands me my change, and I drop the coins into the donation cup.

"Merry Christmas," I say, as I grab my things and head towards the door.

"Hey!" He calls out after me. "You can't say that."

Surprised, I stop and turn around.

"You're supposed to say Happy Holidays." He informs me, and I bristle.

How is it that anyone has ever been offended when people wish them a merry Christmas? Surely they know the intention is good, right? Why take offense, even if you don't believe or celebrate the season? It seems like such a stupid thing to be offended over. And since I'm not one to tiptoe around people's feelings, I give the cashier a flat look. "Right. Sorry. Didn't mean to wish you a Merry Christmas *on* Christmas." I say sarcastically, as I push the door open and step back into the cold.

I grunt as I open my car door, placing everything on the passenger seat before getting in behind the wheel. I start the engine, and the radio blares to life. Instead of music, it's the police officer's interview still playing. *"...We believe he's finding his victims at gas stations and liquor stores..."*

"What is this, The Nightmare Before Christmas?" I mutter, hitting the button to change the station. "Jingle Bells" fills the car, and I find myself humming along as I pull out of the parking lot.

I tap my fingers on the steering wheel to the beat, my head bobbing from side to side as I sing along. My cell phone suddenly rings, and I lean over the passenger seat, stretching to reach it. I glance at my phone. The caller ID reads "Sugarplum." A small smile ghosts my lips, and I'm about to answer it when I happen to glance into my rearview mirror. My mouth drops open as a figure shifts in my backseat. I straighten up, my heart slamming against my ribs. I can hear the blood rushing in my ears. *What the fuck?* A car pulls up directly behind me, its headlights blinding, and I blink against the sudden glare. I fight against the reflected light to get a good look at the person sitting in my car, then do a double-take. My breath catches in my throat.

Santa is sitting in my backseat.

4
HOLLY

Holy shit! Holy shit! Holy Shit!

I twist in my seat, trying to get a clearer view of the figure in the back. The light catches on something plastic. It's a mask. A cheap, plastic Santa mask, the kind you see hanging in dollar stores or plastered on the faces of children. It's fixed in a wide grin, the painted red lips stretched into a permanent smile, but the eyes are just empty holes filled with darkness. A street light shines into the eyes behind the empty holes, and a chill, far deeper than the winter air outside, settles over me.

"Oh my God," I whisper, the words barely escaping my lips. I force my attention back to the road, my hands tightening on the steering wheel, my mind frozen. *Is this really happening?* I glance back and forth between the rearview mirror and the icy road in front of me, but the masked figure in my backseat doesn't move. His perfect stillness makes the hairs on the back of my neck stand on end.

My mind races. *What should I do? Do I pull over? Then what?* I would never be able to outrun him in these heels. I consider dialing 911. *But then what?* No one could get to me in time... I feel a little hysterical and force myself to calm down, suddenly feeling very alone. None of my options are good.

A voice, low and raspy, and way too close to me, cuts through my thoughts.

"Holly Woods?" And even though the voice is low and soft, it sends a jolt of pure, primal fear through me. "You've been naughty," he says.

I decide to pull the car over, my foot instinctively moving towards the brake. I have to get out of here. I have to get away from him. But before I can stop the car, he moves. A blur of red and white as the Santa mask lunges forward. The painted smile seems to widen, to become more menacing as it catches the glare of the headlights coming towards me.

"Ho, ho, ho!" The words are forced and strained, not a laugh at all, but an accusation. He's on me in the next second. His weight pressing against the back of my seat, his hands reaching for me. I see a flash of silver in his right hand—a knife, glinting in the streetlights. Panic explodes in my chest, a cold, suffocating wave of full-fledged and utter panic. I slam on the brakes, the car lurching violently, throwing him forward. He slams against the back of my seat, his masked face inches from mine. The plastic digs into my shoulder. I can smell him now – a mix of sweat and something else... something musty, like old clothes and decay.

Bracing myself, I hit the gas, swerving wildly, trying to get him away from me and to throw him off balance. He grabs the back of my seat, his fingers digging into the leather, pulling himself up. His masked head whips back and forth, as if he's searching for something. *He's lost the knife. Thank God!*

He leans his face forward in between the seats but doesn't reach for me. I glance at him, still swerving, still forcing him to hold onto the seats. His eyes roam over the floor. He's still searching for his knife. He's distracted and in perfect range. I bring my elbow back, connecting with his face, and hear a sickening crack of plastic as the Santa mask splits down one side. He recoils, his head snapping back.

I jerk the steering wheel to one side and put pressure on the brakes, trying to pull over. But he's on me again, his hands snaking around my neck, squeezing. His grip is tight, cutting off my air. My vision spots. I claw at his hands with one of mine, the other still tight on the wheel. The car is barely moving, rolling along as my legs flail. I hit the gas, and the car lurches forward. My assailant's body rears back, but he doesn't let go of the grip he has on my neck. If anything, his grip gets tighter. I scratch at his arms, my nails digging into his skin, then try to hit him, my lungs burning. I gasp, trying to pull in even a little bit of air. I need to breathe.

Desperate, I reach for his face, my fingers grabbing at the front of the mask, finding purchase in the eye holes, and I pull. The mask starts to come off, but he jerks back out of reach, and suddenly I'm free. He carefully readjusts the cracked plastic back over his face as my body heaves in lungfuls of air.

"Dashing through the snow. In a one-horse open sleigh. Over the fields we go," he sings, his voice a distorted, sing-songy whisper, the lyrics of a familiar Christmas carol twisted into something terrifying. "Laughing all the way. Ho, Ho, Ho!"

I'm still gasping in air, trying to restore oxygen to my bloodstream. My vision starts to clear. I tighten my grip on the steering wheel. I consider putting on my seatbelt and planting my car straight into a tree, but there's a good chance I'd get hurt while my attacker would probably be fine in the safety of the back seat. And even if he did get hurt more than me, how would I get home? All I have on are my red heels. If I crash or pull over, I won't be able to outrun him, and it wouldn't be long before I froze to death in my stupid little dress. However, I clearly can't stay here in the car with him. The pain lingering around my neck is making that abundantly clear.

I look back over my shoulder, wondering what he's doing, when suddenly he swings his fist at me. I barely have time to look away before the back of his fist connects with the side of my face. Pain explodes behind my eye, a blinding flash of white-hot agony. My head snaps sideways, hitting the window with a sickening crack. The world tilts, and then everything goes dark.

I slump against the door, my hands falling limply from the steering wheel, my foot pressing down on the gas pedal. The car lurches forward again, the engine roaring.

Through a haze of pain, I hear him swear, then feel him moving, hear the rustle of his clothes as he reaches over me and grabs the steering wheel, his masked face contorted in concentration as he fights to control the now wildly speeding car. I struggle to stay conscious, my head throbbing, blood trickling down my temple, blurring my vision. My eyes flutter open again, and I see him, his focus entirely on the road, his hands gripping the wheel tightly. *Guess I almost put us into that tree after all.*

I shake my head, trying to clear the fog, trying to fight back the darkness. My foot is still on the gas, the car accelerating. I try to free it, but my leg stays heavy and unresponsive. And then I see it. The knife. It's under my feet, half-hidden in the shadows.

I suddenly feel overly alert. Slowly, I reach down to the car floor, my heart pounding as my fingers scramble for the weapon. I keep my head against the car door, and my eyes mostly closed, trying not to alert the killer above me to the fact that I am awake. I glance up, but his focus is on the road ahead of us. I silently pray that he is doing a good job steering. I don't dare let up on the gas pedal. I peek down at my feet. *Where is the damn knife?* I can't quite reach it. I lean forward... almost have it... There! I've got it. I look up to find his dark, empty eyes on me.

His head tilts slightly, the jovial Santa mask now seeming to leer, and then he reaches for the knife. I react on instinct, pure adrenaline surging through me. I slam my foot down on the brake, the car screeching as it comes to a sudden halt, and at the same moment, I yank the knife out of his reach. He flies forward, slamming into the dashboard with a dull thud.

I bring the knife up, my hand shaking, aiming for him. He twists away at the last second, and the blade only catches the side of his face, tearing a long, bloody gash along his cheek and piercing his ear. He lets out a guttural cry, a sound that's more animal than human.

"Naughty!" He shouts.

My head is throbbing, the side of my face sticky with blood from where I hit the window. I try to open the door, but it's locked. *Think!* I frantically try to remember where the unlock button is, my fingers fumbling blindly. Too late.

He grabs my arm, his grip like a vise. I pull the knife back, out of his reach, as my fingers finally find the unlock button. I press it, and the sound of the doors unlocking reverberates around me.

The psycho Santa Claus... *What were they calling him? The Kris Kringle Killer?*... grabs for my hand, the one still clutching the knife. I swing it at him, slashing wildly, the blade slicing through the air. A guttural cry, a noise I've never made before, escapes me.

He lunges for me, and I slam on the gas, throwing us both back into our seats. I raise the knife above him and thrust it down as hard as I can, but he catches my arm, his strength surprising. I'm still holding onto the steering wheel; some part of me can't let it go. With one hand, I steer, keeping us on the road, and with the other, I try again and again to stab the man in my front seat, but he's too strong, and he's got two hands. I scream as I feel him wrenching the knife from my grip. I slam on the brakes, and he flies forward, nearly rolling off the front seat. He catches himself with one hand on the floor of the car, his legs flailing above the center console.

He pushes himself up off the floor, frantically brushing his long, stringy hair out of his face. He sits up sideways in the passenger seat, and I stare. His mask—the plastic mask—is on the floor of my car, and underneath it he's wearing full face makeup.

His face is an unnatural white, his cheeks and lips a bright, rosy red. White eyebrows cover his own, and long, doll-like lashes have been drawn around his eyes. He looks... ridiculous. Pathetic. And yet, still terrifying. Even more disturbing, he has a Santa Claus beard on UNDER the mask. *Who is this psycho?*

He grabs his face, feels his flesh, and starts to scream. "No! No! No! No! NO!" I guess he's feeling exposed. He suddenly flings an arm across the space between us and smacks my hand, the one holding the knife. The knife flies into the back seat in a flash of silver. *Shit!* I slam my foot down on the gas, swerving wildly, desperate to keep him off balance. He's sort of lying in the passenger seat, his feet over the center console, his back against the passenger side door. He grabs onto the seatback with one hand and the dashboard with the other, his legs up in the air, like a turtle on its back. *It's now or never!*

I take my foot off the gas and pull my leg up into my seat, my short dress easily giving way. Using the steering wheel, I lift myself up and, reaching across the space, kick him right in the face. His head rears back, connecting with the car door behind him. I kick him again and again, then, reaching across him, I pull the passenger door handle. The door swings open behind him. He manages to hold on, clinging to the car seat. I kick him again, kicking and pushing at him with all my strength as the car drifts aimlessly, moving at a crawl.

"Get. Out. Get. Out. Get! Out!" I scream, my voice hoarse and ragged.

I kick him one last time, the impact bruising my heel, then, with a primal shriek, I push. His grip on the dashboard slips. He tries to recover by grabbing the back seat, but he misses, tumbling out of the car and rolling across the pavement. I leap back into my seat and stomp on the gas pedal. The vehicle swerves violently, the open door slamming shut. The tires squeal as I accelerate, leaving his body lying in the street.

5
KRIS

Asphalt scrapes across my cheek, smearing my makeup as I fall out of Mother's car and into the street. She doesn't come help me like she used to. There are no words of comfort, no warm hugs. Just the sound of screeching tires as she drives away. *Naughty.* The word echoes in the hollow chambers of my mind, a constant, grating hum.

She kicked me. It wasn't like Mother to be violent. My brow crinkles. Maybe she doesn't know I'm trying to make it better. *Or maybe Dad was right.* I push the thought away. Mommy was naughty but not mean like Dad. She never hit.

I push myself up, the world tilting precariously, the stars swirling in a dizzying dance. My head hurts. I watch Mom's car disappear in a blur of red taillights. "Nooo!" I scream after the car as it disappears around a bend. *Mom! Don't leave me!*

I shake my head, trying to clear it. No. Not Mom. Mother would never leave me. *Holly.* A sneer fills my face at the name. She thinks she can live in my house and replace Mother. She thinks she can cheat and get away with it, but Santa knows where you are sleeping. I start to hum the special words to Dad's song. "He sees why you're awake. He knows that you've been bad, not good..." And Holly was bad.

I whimper softly, suddenly thinking about Mother. *She left me.* I peer down the road where her car had disappeared. I had planned to go home with her. We were going to go together, and I was going to make it better. *No blood this time.* But she'd been naughty, and now I had to get home on my own. I look for my sleigh and reindeer, but I haven't been able to find them for days now. Shouldn't they be here? Helping me? "Do I have to do it all myself?" I scream at the night sky, holding my hurting head. A sob escapes me.

"Stop crying, you little pussy!" Dad's voice fills my mind. *"Stop whimpering! Be a man."* I cringe away from the voice. *She left me!* I want to tell Dad, but he's suddenly not there, and his absence is worse than the voice. All alone.

The air is frigid as I start walking toward my childhood home. What choice do I have? White clouds form in front of my face as I breathe, and I make a game of blowing and then walking through the mist. As I trudge through the wet snow, the urge to run back to the asylum creeps up on me. I could just walk into the nearest police station, and they'd put me back in my nice padded cell. Dad's voice is unusually silent as I contemplate this plan of action. I wait for him to tell me that I'm being a pussy and to be a man and do my job, but he doesn't.

I stop. I could go. I've done so much already. I don't have to go kill Mother. Even if it would make the memories better. I hesitate, filled with indecision, but then my shoulders droop. I would always feel incomplete. I would know... *know* that I hadn't done my job as Santa. Resignation overwhelms me. *Have to punish the naughty. Have to punish the naughty. It's what naughty girls get for Christmas. ...And Mom was naughty.*

I don't tell Dad that I plan to make it nicer. I've been doing it his way, with all the blood, but for Mom, I plan to do it differently.

My boots crunch on the gravel and then in the snow, the sound a steady, rhythmic cadence in the silence of the night. The raindrops turn into big, fluffy snowflakes as the road stretches out before me, a dark ribbon winding through the desolate landscape. The moon hangs high in the sky, a pale, watchful eye.

My mind drifts back to the day I left the asylum. I'd gone home. I always go home. To my surprise, Mother had been there, sleeping. She had a new son. He'd been asleep in my bed. A small sob escapes me. *She replaced me!* She also had a new husband. Dad's voice is suddenly back with a vengeance. "She's naughty!" He says emphatically, and I cringe. "Your mom's bad, Kris! Naughty!"

Dad had been right all along. Mom was naughty. I knew as soon as I saw her that she was bad. It was easy to tell. Santa knows if you've been bad or good... I had hoped she was good. That Dad was wrong. But he'd been right. Mom was definitely sleeping with another man.

How could she replace me? The thought burns through my mind, leaving me feeling raw. The picture of Mom lying on the carpet as her blood spills all around her, a large dark pool... Mom died and left me. Then Dad left me, too. *Everybody leaves me.*

After that, I went to work. Santa had to punish the naughty. I'd saved Mom for last, for Christmas Eve. I wanted it to be special... different... to do it better. I hated remembering all the blood, and I burned with shame whenever I remembered how I'd pulled away from her. This time, I would hold her, comfort her, be there for her as she peacefully went to sleep... forever. Tears pour down my face at the thought of Mom leaving me again, but what can I do? She was naughty, and someone had to punish the naughty.

I sigh and pick up my pace. No point in lolligagging, as Mom would say.

6
HOLLY

The fluorescent lights of the interrogation room hum overhead, casting a harsh, sterile glow on everything. I sit across the steel table from two uniformed officers, the cheap coffee in the Styrofoam cup doing little to warm or calm me down. My face throbs, a dull ache radiating from the bandaged cut on my temple, and I can still taste the metallic tang of blood in my mouth. I just want to go home.

"I told you," I repeat, my voice flat, exhausted. "He was already in the car."

Officer Cane, a man with a perpetually skeptical expression, leans forward. "And this is the best description you can give us?"

"What do you want from me?" I snap, the weariness giving way to a flicker of anger. "He was wearing a mask. A Santa mask. And when the mask finally came off, he had a fake beard and makeup on *underneath the mask*. How am I supposed to know what he actually looks like? I told you exactly where I left him. Just go get him!"

Officer Shepherd, younger but still with gray in his beard, answers almost nonchalantly. "We sent a car. He wasn't there." He shrugs.

I stare at him, the odd desire to punch him in the face almost overwhelming. Fury fills me. "You let him get away?" I ask incredulously. "Perfect." I stand up, the chair scraping against the linoleum floor. "Well, this has been a spectacular waste of time," I say, my voice dripping with anger and... panic? "I'm sure that in the two and a half hours you've kept me here, he's found his next victim and killed her. So glad I took the time on Christmas Eve to come in."

I turn to leave.

"Where do you think you're going?" Cane asks, his voice sharp.

"Home."

"We aren't finished yet."

"I can assure you..." I begin, but the door opens, and an older man in casual clothes steps into the room. He shuts the door behind him, the click of the lock echoing in the small space.

"Mrs. Woods?" he asks, his voice calm, steady.

"Yes?" I answer, my voice biting.

"I'm Detective Donner." He gives me a brief, assessing look. Then a quick smile. "Can you confirm for me that you live at 3617 Mistletoe Lane?"

"Yes," I say, irritated. I've already answered these questions.

He gives me a peculiar look, a flicker of something I can't quite place in his eyes.

"Why?" I ask, my voice sharper now.

Officer Cane, who was sitting behind the desk, stands and gets out of the way as Donner moves toward him. Donner sits down at the desk, the metal chair squeaking beneath his weight. "Have a seat, Mrs. Woods."

"No, thank you," I say, my voice tight. "I've wasted enough time..."

Donner ignores me, slapping a mug shot onto the table. It's a grainy black-and-white photo of a young man. He looks normal if a little too happy. He seems almost gleeful in the photo.

"Was this the man who attacked you?"

They have a picture? I've been here for two hours trying to describe him, and they have a picture? I pick up the photo, my stomach churning. It's... vaguely familiar, but the mask... the makeup... "I... maybe," I say slowly, shaking my head. "You think this is him?"

"Seven years ago," Donner says, his voice flat, emotionless, "officers picked up a man at your address wearing a Santa suit, hat, and beard. Called himself Kris Kringle. He'd killed the couple who lived there because they were..." He makes air quotes with his fingers. "...naughty.'"

A chill runs through me. "That's what my guy said to me."

"When we looked into it," Donner continues, "we found that both of them were having affairs. Along with every victim in the last eleven days."

I stare at him, bewildered, confused. "Okay...?"

"He said it was his job, as Santa, to punish those on his 'naughty list.'"

Officer Cane interjects, "A vigilante Santa Claus."

Donner doesn't even glance at him. "Shut up, Cane."

Cane coughs, but looks unapologetic. "Yes, sir."

"The guy's real name is Kris Conners," Donner continues. "Apparently, he grew up in your house. Lived there until his Dad murdered his mother on Christmas Eve after finding out that she was having an affair. Officers arrested his Dad, and Kris was put into the system..."

I listen with growing dread. "And you think that's..." I gesture to the photo. "...who attacked me tonight?"

"We do."

"How is he... Shouldn't he be in prison?"

"Kris Conners escaped two weeks ago," Donner says, "when he was being transported from one asylum to another."

And then it hits me. "Wait," I say, my voice agitated. "He grew up in my house?"

"If you could tell us..." Donner begins.

I stand abruptly, the chair scraping against the floor. "Are you saying this psychopath knows where I live?" Panic claws at me, a cold, suffocating wave. My heart pounds in my chest, a frantic drumbeat against my ribs. *Beau. Barry.*

"Sit down," Donner says, his voice firm. "We're not done here."

I grab my purse, slinging it over my shoulder and turning to leave. Officer Thistle, a young woman with a determined set to her jaw, steps in front of me, holding up a hand to stop me.

"Get out of my way," I say, my voice low and dangerous, my fingers curling into my palm.

Thistle hesitates, backing off slightly, but still blocking my path. I try to move past her again.

"Mrs. Woods!" Donner's voice is sharp, commanding.

I whirl about to face him. "Have you sent someone to check on my family?" I ask, my voice panicked and oddly high-pitched.

There's an uncomfortable pause as Donner exchanges a quick glance with Officer... *Shepherd was it?* Shepherd gives a discreet but still noticeable shake of his head. They haven't sent anyone.

"This is unbelievable," I breathe, the words laced with disbelief and growing terror. I reach for the door handle, yanking it open. Thistle steps in front of me again.

"Get out of my way," I repeat, my voice loud, but dead calm.

"Mrs. Woods, if you could just..." Donner begins.

I turn to face him, my eyes blazing. "I handed this asshole to you on a silver platter, and you let him get away," I say, each word clipped and precise. "And then you have the balls to sit here and tell me my family is probably in danger, while you interrogate me like I'm some sort of criminal?"

I take a step closer to him, my voice dropping to a near whisper. "Detective, if my family has even had to lock the doors to feel safe, I will make it my mission in life to ruin you."

I turn and walk out of the room, Thistle finally stepping aside.

"Let's get some people to her house, shall we?" Donner says, his voice tight.

"Yes, sir," Shepherd replies, fumbling for the walkie-talkie on his shoulder. "All available units, I need all available units at 3617 Mistletoe Lane. Repeat, all available units..."

Donner hurries out the door after me. "Mrs. Woods! Mrs. Woods!"

I stop reluctantly, turning to face him.

"What is your name, Detective?" I ask, my voice flat.

"Donner. Detective Donner. Are you asking so you know who to file your complaints against?" He offers a weak smile, but I don't even blink.

"I'm asking so I know who to hold responsible should anything have happened to my family in my absence." My voice is icy, unwavering.

"Mrs. Woods," Donner says, his voice taking on a sharper edge, "This particular killer only targets people, well, women, who are having an affair. So, is there anything I should know about?"

"Like what?" I ask, not trying to be obtuse. My mind just isn't functioning like it should.

"Like... are you having an affair?" Donner asks, his eyes boring into mine. "Because if you aren't, we should have nothing to worry about."

I stare at him for a moment, my brain processing too much information. And then the world comes back into focus, crisp and clear.

"Right," I say, my voice dripping with sarcasm. "Because psychopaths who escape asylums are always so logical."

Donner doesn't know what to do with that, and before he can ask me his question again, I take a step towards him. "If you're not going to do anything useful," I continue, my voice rising with anger, "the least you can do is get out of my way."

"I already have units on their way to your address," Donner says, his voice tight.

"Already?" I repeat, the sarcasm heavy in my voice.

We stand there, locked in a silent confrontation, the tension between us thick enough to cut with a knife. Finally, I push past him.

"You should at least go to a hospital," Donner calls after me.

I don't even pause as I lift my middle finger into the air, flipping him the bird without looking back.

"We're all going to the same..." He sighs. "Here! I'll drive you!" He shouts as he runs to catch up to me.

7
HOLLY

The quiet of our street is shattered by the arrival of the police. Multiple cars screech to a halt in front of our house, tires spitting gravel onto the snow-covered lawn. The flashing red and blue lights paint the night in a chaotic glow. Two officers, their hands instinctively hovering near their weapons, move with practiced efficiency up the front steps. Two more disappear around the side of the house, heading for the back. A cold dread settles in my stomach as Detective Donner pulls his shop up to my driveway. I open the door before he stops moving and exit the vehicle, finding it hard to breathe.

The events of the night replay in my mind, a terrifying loop of a masked face, and a hard, constricting pressure on my throat. It's snowing big, fat flakes —the kind that stick to the ground and turn into inches. I stumble out of the car, my legs shaky, desperate to see Barry, to see Beau, to confirm with my own eyes that they are safe.

Officer Shepherd, the one who had shrugged earlier while admitting that they had failed to catch my attacker, steps in front of me, effectively blocking my path to the house. *What is it with everyone blocking my way today?*

"Ma'am, I'm gonna need you to wait here," he says, his voice firm, but not unkind.

"Get out of my way!" I try to push past him, my hands clenched into fists, but he stands his ground, an immovable barrier of blue uniform.

"Ma'am, it's for your own safety." His words, meant to reassure, only fuel my growing panic. Did that mean my family *was* in danger?

I strain to see past him, to peer through the living room window, but the curtains are drawn, the house shrouded in darkness. The two officers at the front door are peering through the side windows, their faces etched with concern, their movements hesitant.

Enough of this bullshit!

Without warning, I push Officer Shepherd into the snow drift beside him. I manage to catch him off guard, and all 6 feet of him falls into the snow. I rush past him, aware of Detective Donner behind me. "Please..." I whisper as I race up the icy steps to my front door. My voice cracking, tears stinging my eyes. "Please."

Officer Thistle steps in front of my front door and puts a hand up to block me, the same way she had in Donner's office. I practically growl at her. "Move!" I say, my voice trembling with suppressed rage, "or you're going to lose an arm."

Detective Donner appears behind me, his face drawn and serious. "It's okay, Thistle. Let her through," he says, his eyes meeting mine, a flicker of something that might be understanding in their depths.

I push past her, my breath catching in my throat as I burst into the house. "Barry? Beau?" I call out, my voice echoing in the sudden silence.

I stop short, my hand flying to my mouth. The living room is bathed in the warm, comforting glow of the Christmas tree lights. Barry is on the couch, Beau nestled securely in his arms, playing contentedly with a small toy truck. He looks up, his face lighting up with a broad, innocent smile when he sees me.

"Mommy!" he cries, scrambling off Barry's lap and running towards me, his small feet pattering across the hardwood floor.

"Hi, baby!" I say, my voice choked with tears of relief. I bend down and scoop him up into my arms, holding him tight, burying my face in the sweet scent of his hair. Relief washes over me, so intense it almost makes me weak in the knees. *They're safe. They're both safe.*

I kiss the top of his head, but he squirms in my arms, eager to show me something.

"Look, Mom! Look what I got!" He holds up the toy truck, shiny and new, its chrome gleaming in the Christmas tree lights.

Barry joins us, a small, relieved smile playing on his lips. "He couldn't wait any longer," he says, his eyes meeting mine.

I give Beau another squeeze, the urge to be close to him overwhelming. "Do you like it?" I ask, my voice soft and tired.

"So cool!" he exclaims, his eyes wide with excitement.

"So cool!" I echo, trying to mirror his enthusiasm and push away a sudden overwhelming feeling of exhaustion. I suddenly feel shaky. Beau squirms to be let down, and I set him gently on the floor. I watch as he runs back to the couch, completely engrossed in his new toy, the small plastic wheels rolling across the cushions.

Barry steps closer, his eyes examining the bandage on my forehead, his brow furrowed with concern. "You okay?" he asks, his voice low and filled with worry.

I nod, managing a weak smile. "Yes." But then I look up at him and catch a glimpse of something in his eyes... Was that fear? He'd been genuinely worried about me. I can't remember the last time Barry concerned himself with my well-being. But I'm too tired. It suddenly doesn't matter that it takes a serial killer attacking me to get my husband's attention. The events of the evening have created a temporary truce. We stand there, unsure of what to do. He doesn't wrap me in his arms like I'd like him to, but he doesn't look away either.

Detective Donner approaches, his expression serious but his eyes softer now. "The house is clear," he says, his voice cutting through the quiet. "There's no sign of him." He pauses, his eyes sweeping over the room and the two of us standing there, obviously not touching each other. "I'm going to leave a unit outside, just in case. If you hear or see anything, call us right away. Lock the doors behind us."

"We will," Barry says, his voice firm. "Thank you, Detective."

Donner's gaze lingers on me for a moment, a flicker of something unreadable in his eyes. I return his look coolly, reminding him that he is the one in the wrong here. The one who has, so far, made all the mistakes. He hesitates, then gives a curt nod. "Well, good night," he says.

"Merry Christmas, Detective," Barry says.

Donner turns back towards us. He looks from Barry to me, then back again, a strange, almost searching expression on his face.

"Merry Christmas," he finally murmurs, before turning and leaving. The other officers follow close behind him.

The silence they leave in their wake is deafening. My shoulders slump. I feel like I could lie down on the hardwood floor beneath my feet and sleep for a week. I look at Beau, and the thought of reading him a bedtime story and putting him to sleep makes me want to cry. To my relief, Barry steps in front of me, gently grasps me by one elbow, and points me towards our bedroom. "Why don't you go get cleaned up and changed. I'll put Beau to bed."

I nod gratefully, too tired to argue. I shuffle into our bedroom, dropping my coat, purse, shoes, and finally the stupid little dress in a trail across our bedroom floor. I'll clean up the mess later. All I care about is a shower.

I turn on the hot water and can barely wait for it to get warm before stepping inside. I take down my hair and let the water pour over my head and face. I suddenly feel all the newly acquired aches and bruises as the warm water rushes over my body, trying to wipe them away.

I close my eyes and suddenly see a face in a rearview mirror. My eyes fly open, and I'm back in my shower. Unfortunately, it's no better the next time I close my eyes or the time after that. Each time I close my eyes, his face, the knife, the sound my head made cracking against the car window... It's all right there waiting behind my closed eyelids.

I decide to keep my eyes open. *How am I going to sleep? Especially since he knows where I live.* I struggle to remember if we told Barry that. He needs to know... Needs to know that the killer's dad murdered his mom here on Christmas Eve in our living room. But my brain feels like mush or sludge, whichever is slower.

I stay in the shower so long that my fingers prune. Finally, I find the will to remove myself from the warmth of the water and step out into the cold night air. Even with a heater, it's always cold during winter. Our house is just too big to heat properly. I stand over the little vent, doing its best to heat our bathroom, and luxuriate in the warm air blowing out of it. Somehow, I manage my regular routine, drying myself off, putting lotion on everything, getting dressed, then brushing and drying my hair.

When I finally emerge from our bedroom, Barry and Beau are nowhere to be seen. I know I should go check on Beau, maybe even take over his bedtime routine, but instead, I find myself walking over to the window. I pull back the curtain and press my face close to the glass to block out the glare from the indoor lights.

Fat snowflakes pour down from a dark sky, flashing bright white in the street lights. The houses around us look small and insignificant as the snowfall buries them, turning them into nothing more than large snow drifts. Even the cheerful Christmas lights adorning many of the houses seem muffled under the snow and in the dark, and, even though I'm inside, I know it's one of those quiet nights, where if you stop and listen, the only thing you'll hear is the whisper of the snow falling.

A police cruiser sits parked in our driveway, a silent, watchful presence, but it does little to reassure me. That psycho Santa Claus is still out there, and I can't shake the feeling that he's lurking in the shadows, biding his time until he can get to me. I wonder to myself how long it will be before I feel safe again in my own home.

Barry suddenly comes out of Beau's room, closing the door softly behind him. "Finally got him into bed," he says, a weary smile on his face.

"I can't believe he's still awake," I reply, my voice barely a whisper, my gaze fixed on the police car. "I can barely keep my eyes open."

Barry stops next to me, his shoulder brushing against mine. "You've had a rough night," he says softly, his voice filled with concern.

An awkward silence descends between us, the unspoken tension hanging heavy in the air.

"Why don't I start on the stockings and presents?" Barry suggests, breaking the silence, his voice gentle. "While you go say goodnight? Then we'll get you into bed."

I groan softly, wavering on my feet. "Oh my gosh... presents! I completely forgot," I say, a fresh wave of guilt and exhaustion washing over me. Filling stockings and putting presents under the tree, as if everything is normal, feels like a Herculean task. "Can't Santa Claus do that this year?' I moan. "It *is* supposed to be his job."

Barry chuckles, a warm, familiar sound that momentarily eases the tightness in my chest. "I don't mind helping," he says, his voice softening, his eyes meeting mine. "Especially after getting my own little Christmas miracle."

He looks at me, his eyes filled with a depth of emotion I haven't seen in a long time – relief, gratitude, and something else... something that looks like... hope? "I hate to think what could have happened," he continues, his voice low and sincere. "I know things haven't been... easy lately... but I don't know what I would have done if I had lost you."

He reaches out and takes my hand, his fingers interlacing with mine. I look down at our joined hands, surprised by the simple gesture of affection. It's been so long since he's touched me like this. I look up at him, and our eyes meet, a silent conversation passing between us, a fragile bridge being tentatively rebuilt.

I'm on Sarah's back patio, the air thick with the lazy hum of late summer. Fairy lights twinkle overhead, casting a warm, golden glow on the mismatched collection of patio furniture. Empty pizza boxes and half-eaten bowls of chips litter the glass-topped table. Laughter spills out from our little group, a comfortable, easy sound.

Our friends, Liam and Chloe, sit tangled together on the wicker loveseat, whispering secrets and stealing kisses. Maya and Ben are locked in a fierce but playful debate about some obscure indie band. And I... I was still navigating the tentative landscape of new love with Barry.

Barry was sitting on one of the slightly wobbly metal chairs, his long legs stretched out in front of him, a half-empty beer bottle clutched loosely in his hand. He was quieter than the others, a gentle observer with a dry wit that would occasionally cut through the boisterous chatter, making me laugh until my sides ached. He'd look at me sometimes, a soft smile playing on his lips, a silent understanding passing between us that made me feel like I was the only person in the world he truly saw.

A comfortable silence settles over the patio, and suddenly, the urge to be close to him can't be ignored any longer. Without a word, I walk over to him. He looks up at me with a question in his warm brown eyes, quickly replaced by a gentle welcome. I sit down and curl up in his lap.

His arms wrap around me instinctively, a natural, unthinking gesture as I lean back against his chest, the solid warmth of him a comforting anchor. His chin rests lightly on my shoulder, his breath soft against my hair.

We'd stayed like that for what felt like hours, through the ebb and flow of conversation, sharing silly stories and future dreams. We ate greasy pizza, and laughed at Liam's terrible jokes and Maya's dramatic retelling of a minor work mishap, Barry's quiet laughter a warm rumble beneath me. All the while, I was cocooned in the simple intimacy of being held by him, feeling utterly safe and cherished.

That night on Sarah's patio, surrounded by the laughter of friends and the promise of new love, had felt like the beginning of something real, something lasting.

A longing that I had quietened long ago suddenly sprouts in my chest. *If only you could go back...*

"Go say goodnight," Barry murmurs, squeezing my hand gently, pulling me away from the memories.

I nod, a lump forming in my throat, and turn towards Beau's room. I walk quietly down the hallway, the floorboards creaking under my feet. I go to tap on my son's bedroom door, but think better of it and gently push it open instead. I peek into Beau's bedroom. The soft glow of a miniature Christmas tree perched on his small desk casts long shadows across the wall. A few discarded clothes lie scattered on the floor, a testament to the whirlwind of energy that is a five-year-old. The room is a familiar, comforting space, a stark contrast to the fear I can't quite let go of.

I step inside, careful not to make a sound, and sit gently on the edge of his bed. The mattress dips slightly under my weight. Beau stirs, his eyelids fluttering open. He looks up at me, his face soft and sleepy, a small smile playing on his lips. I run a hand gently through his tousled hair, the simple gesture filling me with a wave of tenderness.

"Sorry, bug," I whisper, my voice thick with emotion. "I didn't mean to wake you. I just wanted to say goodnight." The guilt I've been holding at bay for not being there for him on Christmas Eve, blazes through me. "I'm sorry our Christmas

Eve was ruined," I say lamely, not quite able to take full responsibility like I should.

He blinks sleepily, his gaze focusing on my face. "It's okay, Mom," he mumbles, his voice still heavy with sleep.

He reaches up a small hand and touches the bandage on my forehead, his little fingers tracing the edge of the cut. "Was it scary?" he asks, his voice barely audible.

I nod, smiling so as not to alarm him. "Yeah," I whisper. "But I knew I had to get back here to you and Dad." The smile slips as I try to force the image of a face in a mask out of my mind. "And now the police are right outside, so there's nothing to worry about, okay?"

"Okay," he mumbles, his eyelids drooping again. The simple faith of a child.

"Now, go back to sleep so Santa Claus can come," I whisper, tucking the blanket more snugly around him.

"Okay," he repeats, rolling over and snuggling into his pillow, his breathing already becoming slow and even.

I lean down and kiss him softly on the cheek, the scent of his hair and the warmth of his skin filling me with a fierce protectiveness. I linger there for a moment, watching his peaceful sleep, trying to imprint this image in my mind, a shield against the darkness.

A sudden unease prickles my skin, and I sit up straight, feeling eyes on me. I'm being watched! I glance towards the window and see a shadow move behind the curtain. My heart races as I slowly stand and walk towards it, my breath catching in my throat. I stretch, reaching towards the curtain, and tentatively pull the fabric apart. There's nothing on the other side, just darkness and snowflakes. The peace and normalcy mock my fear. I pull the curtains back together, blocking my view. *Stop it!* I tell myself. *It's just nerves. You're still in shock.* I tell myself.

"Have sweet dreams," I whisper to Beau, my voice barely audible.

"You too," Beau murmurs in his sleep.

I walk to the side of his bed. "Oh, I will," I whisper softly, my gaze lingering on him. "I'll dream of you."

I turn, my gaze drawn back to the window, then make myself walk to the door. I hesitate at the light switch, a sudden reluctance to turn off the light, as if the darkness itself is a threat to us. I take a deep breath, trying to calm my racing heart. "You're *being paranoid,*" I tell myself. *"The police are right outside. We're safe."*

I reach again for the switch and flick it off, plunging the room into darkness. I close the door softly behind me, the click of the latch echoing in the quiet house.

8

DETECTIVE DONNER

A strong sense of deja vu overwhelms me as I stand on the curb of Mistletoe Lane. It's all frighteningly familiar. Snowflakes pile up on my coat sleeves as I numbly look to my right, remembering. I'd stood under that street light right there, my hands covered in blood. That had been seven years ago. The memory of the icy snow scraping across my hands as I'd tried to wash off the blood still felt fresh. The snow had been days old, hard and icy. Still, it had done the trick. As a rookie detective, I'd tried to save the couple inside, both of them with their throats slit. I'd tried to stop the bleeding. It had been a gut reaction, an instinct. I'd been so green. But then, back then, murder wasn't an everyday experience. Experience taught you. You can't bring them back from a wound like that.

At least no one is dead inside. ...So far, I think to myself. *Holly.* She'd fought him off. I wonder briefly if the other victims had all gone quietly. In her report, Holly had claimed that her attacker had a knife, that he'd held it to her throat, and that she'd driven erratically to throw him off balance until he dropped it. She'd ended up getting a hold of the knife herself and had tried to, in her own words, "stab him repeatedly with it."

One side of my mouth lifts into a smile. She's a firecracker, that one. Not many people had the guts to flip me off. My brow furrows as I think about her. So far, Kris hasn't been wrong about any of the women he's murdered... Not that we have any idea how he knows, but somehow, he *does* know when they're cheating on their spouses. True, none of them resembled his mother and lived at his old address. I suppose it's possible he's mistaken about Holly, and that she's innocent as she's claimed. I catch and correct myself. She hasn't actually claimed innocence, merely evaded answering the question. Was that because she was guilty? Or because the question was too absurd to grace with an honest answer? I didn't know, and I probably didn't need to know. Marital issues aside, she was definitely a target.

We'd recovered the knife from her vehicle. We'd be able to confirm the attacker's identity from the fingerprints on the knife, but no one... and I mean no one, was working in this small town over the holiday, serial killer or not. I dig my phone out of my pocket with a sigh. This was not going to go well. I needed someone at the lab to run the prints. I cringe at ruining another person's Christmas Eve, but, hey, I couldn't run the prints, and we needed to know. This was our first break in this case, and even then, having his identity confirmed still wouldn't tell us where the hell he's been hiding.

A quick flash of regret that Holly hadn't succeeded in stabbing this guy washes over me, but I force it down. It wasn't her responsibility to stop him. That was my job. And I was so damn tired of failing at it.

I interrupt John's Christmas Eve celebration because Katie has two small children, and I don't want to tear her away from them. John grumbles a lot, but I hear him get his coat on and head outside. I've already sent an officer to the lab to wait with the knife. I hang up and sigh again, unable to help myself. It was going to be a long night.

Officer Cane walks up to me and brushes some of the snow off my coat. I'm starting to resemble a snowman. The Woods' house is right up against the mountain where the snowfall is unrelenting. It's piling up on the roads and silencing every sound except its own whisper. I shake my head at the realization that if the Kris Kringle Killer does show up tonight, it will be almost impossible to get back up here if it keeps snowing like this. I make a mental note to add chains to my All Wheel Drive shop.

I suddenly realize Cane is talking to me. "What was that?" I ask.

"I said you're gonna get wet if you let it melt on you like that." Cane beats at the hood of my coat, knocking off more of the snow I've become buried under. He continues. "Thistle and Pine drew the short straws. They're staying to keep an eye on the family tonight. Wiseman took the knife to the lab. Do you have someone headed that way?"

I nod, then say, "Yep. John's headed there now."

"Bet he's thrilled about that."

"You're working. I'm working," I say. "We should all be working to take this guy down, holidays or not." And even to my own ears, I sound a little hysterical. I obviously do to Cane as well because he starts making placating motions with his hands.

"I get it, Chief." He holds his arms out wide like he wants to make sure I can see him standing there and understand that he's one of the good guys, sticking it out on Christmas Eve.

"I know you do," I say and then sigh. *This sucks.*

I wrap up my conversation with Cane and walk back to my car, the snow crunching under my boots. I get in and slam the door shut, hoping it will knock some of the snow off my shop. It does, but not enough. Luckily, snow like this is light. I turn on my windshield wipers to high. They hesitate a moment under the weight of the snow before slowly starting to move. Gradually, they pick up speed, scraping back and forth until I can see out a small hole they've cleared across my windshield. Everything else, including my windows and my side mirrors, is still covered in snow, but I just turn the heater on full blast and make sure the defrost is on before pulling out of the driveway.

I think about the knife headed to the lab. "Please give us something we can use," I mutter to myself aloud. I chew on one finger nail as I drive, contemplating what I know about Kris Conners. If I could only figure out what he's going to do next. Is he the kind of guy who finds another victim when he fails? Or does he keep coming for the same girl until he gets her?

My gut tells me he keeps on coming until he gets the one he's after. Especially Holly. There are too many connections; his childhood home, Holly's similarities to his mother, that it's Christmas Eve... It feels like he's saved the best for last. *God, I hope she's the last!*

I start to turn around. I shouldn't be leaving. I should be there in case... *when* he comes for her. I think about how Holly will react to my being in their house on Christmas Eve, and stop. She will not be happy to see me. Thistle and Pine were there. They could keep the family safe... right? Shouldn't I be doing something more useful, like hunting down leads? I inwardly groan. *If only I had any.* At least we had a clue as to where he would be heading tonight. I decide to post Cane and Wiseman down the street from the house as backup for Thistle and Pine.

They could keep an eye on the street. It's a miserable night to be sitting in a car, but I wasn't going to take any chances.

Eventually, I pull into the deserted precinct parking lot, the streetlights casting a harsh glow over the empty parking spaces. The closer I've gotten to the city, the smaller the snowflakes have become, until finally, they are small, separate, little things floating lazily down from the night sky. They fall through the glow of the nearby streetlights, looking a little like bugs.

I head inside, the silence of the empty hallways amplifying the weariness in my bones. The coffee in the breakroom is stale and bitter, doing little to revive me. I sit down at my desk, the metal chair creaking beneath my weight, and stare at the Conners file. Kris' mugshot stares back at me. He looks so normal. Not at all menacing. *How could this guy have murdered all those women?* This psycho thinks he's doing the world a service if his file is to be believed.

I sit back, the creak of my chair overly loud in the silence. I decide to go through it all again while I wait for Cane and Wiseman to arrive with the lab results. I shuffle through the file on my desk, laying out the gruesome pictures again, one by one, staring at the faces of the people I've failed. I comb through every scene, cross-check connections between the women, and even go back over what I know about Kris. Finally, I shake my head. If there is a clue here, I just can't see it.

9
KRIS

Red and blue lights pulse against the snow, a frantic heartbeat against the stillness of the night. I watch the figures jump out of their cars and race up to the house, wondering why they're here. They're early. *I haven't left them a doll yet.* I stand in the shadows of the neighbor's house, leaning against the tan brick, watching them. My friend Cinnamon had lived here. She'd been nice. She'd played hide and seek and tag with me. I'd secretly hoped that she would be my first kiss, but then I was taken away. I make a mental note to check the nice list to make sure she's on it. She deserves presents. Not to be punished.

"Naughty," I say out loud, as I watch the policemen wander in and around home. Mom will be mad — all those wet boots on her hardwood floor.

"Mother," the word comes out of me as a sob. The last time I came home, I'd been looking for her. I'd had to punish the people who thought they could live there instead of Mom and Dad. They'd been naughty.

The image of Mom bleeding out on the living room rug fills my mind, and I whimper. The image feels fresh this close to home. *Mom? Mommy!* I reach for her in my mind, but Dad's voice stops me. *Your Mom is bad, Kris. She's bad!*

That was why I'd had to come. She had to be punished. I cringe away from Dad's voice, trying to hide. I don't tell Dad that I plan to do it nicer this time. He'll be mad, but I don't care. Dad wasn't here, and I was going to fix it. I giggle, feeling a little naughty myself at hiding things from Dad, but I have to. Dad is scary when he's mad.

I shift my feet in the snow. My pants are wet up to my knees, my toes freezing in my boots. It had been a very long walk here. *Where are those reindeer with that sleigh?* No matter. I am here now. I can't wait to get inside. It will be nice and warm inside, with the fire roaring in the fireplace and Mom and Dad sitting on the couch, watching me sift through the presents under the tree. I smile at the thought of all of us safe at home, and then my brow furrows. I shake my head as a thought intrudes. *No, Mom is dead. Dad isn't here. It's Holly. And she's been naughty.*

I growl low in my throat. *Why? Why hadn't she been good?* She was the reason I had to come. *So naughty!* I glare at the house, at the woman inside. She was naughty, just like Mom. Dad had been relentless. *Kris, it's time to do your duty, son. I can't be Santa now; it's up to you.* I hadn't wanted to come. I'd cried and begged, but that had just made Dad mad, his voice getting louder and more insistent, like a ringing in my brain that had made me want to dig it out of my skull. But instead, I'd finally decided to do my job. I'd left the comfort and safety of the asylum to once again be Santa Claus.

I watch as the detective stops on the curb. He looks at the streetlight, really looks at it, and, for a minute, the look in his eyes makes me think he's noticed me, but he doesn't move —

just stands there, his brow furrowed. Another officer walks up to him, and he sort of wakes up. They talk for a moment, then get into their separate cars and drive away.

The last two officers get into the same vehicle. I wait for it to start, for the headlights to come on, and for them to drive away, but they just stay there parked out front. *Why aren't they leaving?* Their presence becomes a dull, irritating hum, like a trapped insect inside my mind. I shift, a silent shadow, and slide deeper into the darkness, feeling impatient. *What do I do?*

Kill them, Kris. Dad's voice intrudes on my thoughts like it so often does. *They're naughty. They took me away. They took me away on Christmas Eve. You never even got to open all of your presents. They hauled you off, and that was the last time you can ever remember being happy. Isn't that right, Kris?*

It was.. After that day, happiness became a distant memory, like love and safety. I look at the cop car again as my temperature rises. Rage pulses through me like it's in my veins.

I move out of the shadows and relative safety of Cinnamon's house and into the falling snow, stalking across a white backdrop and into my own backyard. I peek in through a window and stop short. Mother is there putting me to sleep. She's bent low, kissing my cheek. I put a hand on the window, as a sharp stab of longing and anger shoots through me. But then she sits up, and it's not Mother, it's *her*. *Holly*. The rage returns. I'd been robbed of moments like this because women like her were so naughty!

I step away from the window and stalk around the side of the house. I can see the cop car sitting silently in the driveway, the snow piling higher and higher, blocking the view out the back window. I don't even creep, just walk up to the back of the car, my black shiny Santa boots crunching in the snow. I stop near the back of the car, unsure how to proceed. Everything is so quiet. I'm like the snow itself moving through a winter wonderland. Suddenly, the passenger car door flies open and an officer, one I vaguely recognize, jumps out of the vehicle.

"It's him," I hear him shout as he lunges towards me. But I bring up my knife and slash hard. The officer grabs his neck, gurgling on his own blood as his steps falter. The other officer pokes her head up above the car. Her eyes bulge as blood sprays across the snow. She reaches for her walkie-talkie, but I waggle a finger at her. "Uh, uh uh! What would Santa say?" But she doesn't stop. I hear the button click, and she's about to speak when I throw the knife at her. She shrieks, dodging behind the car to avoid being hit. Without a thought for the man bleeding out at my feet (he was naughty), I race forward, slide across the hood of the car, and land on the other side, almost on top of the other officer. She shrieks again and drops her radio. She'd been trying to call someone again!

"Naughty!" I tell her emphatically, as I wrap my hands around her neck. She points her gun at me, but I knock it out of her grasp with one hand, keeping the other on her soft flesh. I can feel how easy it would be to crush her windpipe, but she's nice. Santa knows these things. So I simply hold her like that, my hands tight around her neck, until she falls asleep. She falls limp in my arms, and I'm pleased with the result. She's so innocent looking, so vulnerable, but no blood. Yes, very happy with it indeed!

Gently, I pick her up and put her back into the front seat of the car. It's freezing outside, and I don't want her catching a cold. I situate her so that she'll be comfortable. I always like placing my dolls. Mother would have been proud of me. She always said a woman should look her best. This doll is pretty, and I want her to look her best when they find her, although she will probably be awake by then. I take my time placing her anyway. It calms me. I gently stroke her cheek, wishing I had time to put on her makeup, but no matter, she wasn't a real doll anyway. There would be time to make a real doll tonight.

I sigh, and it's filled with regret. Let's get this over with. I stand and walk around the car to the dead body bleeding into the snow.

10

HOLLY

Leaving Beau's door slightly ajar, I step out into the living room, the carpet cushioning my steps. The scent of pine needles and Cinnamon hangs in the air, a reminder of the holiday spirit that's been violently disrupted.

I stop at the Christmas tree, my gaze caught by the presents nestled beneath its branches. I look towards the fireplace, at the three stockings hanging heavily from the mantlepiece, overflowing with small gifts and treats. A faint smile touches my lips. It's a scene of domestic warmth and joy, a vivid contrast to the adrenaline still running through my veins. I take a deep breath, trying to calm my nerves. The incident in Beau's room still has me feeling like I'm being watched.

I take another deep breath, trying to shake the feeling, and head into the kitchen, my slippered feet making a soft woosh, woosh noise on the hardwood floor. I pull open a bottom cupboard, the hinges creaking slightly in the quiet house. I pause, looking over my shoulder, listening for any indication that I'm not alone. The silence is broken only by the distant hum of the refrigerator. Reassured, I pull out a large cardboard box.

I carry it carefully to the fireplace and set it on the floor with a soft thud. Kneeling beside it, I pull out a few last-minute additions for the stockings, focusing on the one with Barry's name written in glittery gold letters. I add a small bottle of his favorite cologne, a bag of gourmet coffee, and a small black pocket knife. I smile with satisfaction and carry the box back to the cupboard, slip it inside, and close the door quietly. Standing up, I look in the direction of our bedroom.

"Barry?" I call out softly, my voice echoing slightly in the quiet house. There's no reply. My brow furrows in consternation. *Maybe he's in the bathroom? Maybe he fell asleep.* I stamp down the twinge of annoyance at the thought, after all, he did help, and it is late.

I walk towards the bedroom. "Barry, did you fall asleep?" I call out, a touch louder this time. I try to keep the annoyance out of my voice, but it would have been nice if he'd waited for me.

I round the corner and step into our bedroom. My breath catches, a choked gasp, as I stop short. I blink, my mind not quite processing the nightmare in front of me. The moon filtering through the window is my only source of light, but it's enough. Barry is sitting in a chair by the window, his head slumped forward, his body still. He's either unconscious... or dead. Kris looms over him, his hands pulling on the end of the rope that is wrapped around Barry and the chair, binding him. Not dead then. *Why would he tie up a corpse?*

As he finishes his task, giving the ropes a final tug to ensure they're secure, his voice booms through the room in song. "God rest ye merry gentlemen, let nothing you dismay." His Santa suit is filthy, and... wet? *Did he walk here?* The bloody gash on his cheek is still visible, a stark reminder of our struggle. His hair hangs around his shoulders, wet and stringy, and his makeup is smeared and ghastly. The Joker from the old Batman movies springs to mind. This lunatic laughing with glee as he sings and does a little dance, is a dead ringer for the Joker... with the same disregard for human life.

I stare at him, my mouth open, my heart pounding in my chest.

"Holly Woods." He says it like my name is a dirty word, his voice rising slightly, a hint of manic glee creeping into it. "You're on my naughty list." He points a gloved finger at me, the gesture sending a shiver of fear down my spine. "You've been naughty."

He takes a step towards me, and I instinctively back away, my eyes fixed on him, my mind racing.

"Naughty!" he shouts, making me jump.

I continue to back away from him, my eyes darting around the room. I need something... a weapon. But there's nothing nearby. Only air and a bed. *Could I cover him with a blanket? Stupid.* I am not leaving Barry to suffer the machinations of this psycho path, but... *I can't just stand here.* I glance towards the doorway, calculating the distance, wondering if I can make a break for it.

He smiles and waggles his finger at me, a grotesque parody of a scolding Santa. "Uh, uh, uh," he chides, his voice a sing-songy whisper, and then he turns his back on me and takes a step towards Barry. All thoughts of escape flee, and I follow after him like a puppy, my fear replaced with desperation. "Don't hurt him!" I beg, but it sounds like an order. I will not tolerate him hurting Barry.

Kris looks at me, confused for a moment, as if I've said something insane. Then, his eyes widen as he points to Barry. "Barry's been a good little boy all year," he says, his voice suddenly booming, and I somehow understand that it's the voice he uses when he's *being* Santa Claus. Then, just like that, his expression falls into a mask of exaggerated sadness. He shakes his head slowly, his eyes meeting mine. "But you..." He says, his voice dropping to a whisper. "Ho, ho, ho!"

The way he says it... not a laugh, but an insinuation. He'd said it the same way in the car. My chin lifts defiantly, despite the fear that's gripping me. "What's that supposed to be?" I ask, my voice trembling slightly. "Some sort of accusation?" He walks towards me, his steps slow and deliberate, his eyes never leaving mine. "Ho, ho, ho," he repeats, his voice firmer this time. I try to interrupt him. "If he's nice," I plead, pointing to Barry, "let him go." But Kris just points at me, his eyes filled with a dark, unsettling glee. "Ho, ho, ho," he repeats, again and again, as he stalks toward me. I only feel relief as he moves away from Barry, as he backs me up against the wall.

"You don't know what you're talking about," I insist, again interrupting his litany of Ho! Ho! Ho's! "I'm not a ho."

Kris looks chagrined, shaking his head slightly and looking at me as if I'm the crazy one. Then he starts singing again. "He knows that you've been bad, not good." It takes me a minute to understand what he's saying, and then it clicks.

"You are not Santa Claus, you psycho!" I say, my voice filled with derision. *Seriously? This guy thinks he knows if someone is bad or good?*

A maniacal gleam enters Kris's eyes. "I saw mommy... underneath the mistletoe..." he says, holding a pretend sprig of mistletoe between his fingertips and waving it above my head.

"What are you talking about?" I ask, pushing away the hand hovering uncomfortably close to my face.

"I saw mommy..." he continues, the words taking on a sinister, suggestive tone, as he reaches towards me again, this time towards my stomach as if he intends to tickle me.

"I am not your mother!" I shout, my voice filled with desperate denial. "Look, I know what happened... I know about your Mom..."

Kris moves closer, his face inches from mine, his voice dropping to a low, menacing growl as he sings, "He knows where you are sleeping. He sees why you're awake. He knows that you've been bad, not good. Shoulda been good *for your life's sake*." He takes a step away from me, continuing the song with a flourish. "Oooooooh! You gotta watch out, if you don't want to die..."

"That's not how the song goes," I counter, my voice defiant.

"He makes a list, checks it twice. He already knows who's naughty or nice," he counters, as if he's enjoying himself.

"Recheck your list," I say, my voice rising angrily, despite the terror that's gripping me. "I'm on the nice list.

All the dancing has created some space between us, and I'm feeling pretty confident that if I run, Kris will follow. *Barry, wake up!* I silently pray, as my eyes dart to the doorway, measuring the distance. I glance at Kris and decide to go for it. I push off the wall, racing for the exit, but before I've taken two steps, he lunges after me, his movements surprisingly quick. I try to duck to the side, but he's too fast. He grabs me around the waist, pulling me back and pushing me roughly against the wall. His hands wrap around my neck, squeezing and cutting off my air supply. I guess we're done singing and dancing.

I claw at his hands, desperate to break his grip, but they're like iron bands around my throat. I grab his hair and pull, but he doesn't release me. I reach, trying to gouge out his eyes, but he shifts away, straightening both arms and keeping me at arm's length. My vision starts to blur. Black spots dance in front of my eyes. I gasp for air, but none comes. I feel lightheaded, my strength fading. Finally, in a desperate move, I wedge one leg between us, placing my foot against his stomach. I have the room because he's got me at arm's length. With a surge of adrenaline, I push hard.

Kris stumbles back, releasing his grip on my neck. I gasp, sucking in air, my lungs burning.

Move! I tell myself, and I stumble towards the doorway, my legs weak and unsteady.

Kris pulls a knife out of his belt, the blade glinting in the dim light, and follows me, his eyes fixed on me with a chilling intensity.

I reach the doorway, my hands grasping the frame for support. I'm moving faster now, adrenaline fueling me, but then I freeze.

"Mom?" Beau's small, scared voice.

My heart plummets at the sight of my son standing in the small space that is the entryway to my bedroom. "Beau, go to your room!" I shout, my voice hoarse from my throat being crushed just the moment before. "Right now! Go to your room and lock the door!"

He doesn't move, just stands there, his mouth agape, his eyes wide with terror, staring at the bizarre Santa Claus figure looming behind me. All thoughts of fleeing disappear. I grab onto both sides of the doorway, making myself a barricade across the opening.

"Mom?" Beau whispers again, his voice trembling.

"Go to your room!" I repeat, my voice desperate. "Run!"

Kris tries to push past me, a strange smile spreading across his face. I push against him with all my weight, trying to force him back into the bedroom with Barry, but he doesn't budge. His voice takes on that deep booming quality, his grotesque imitation of Santa Claus. "Well, well, well, what have we here?" he asks, as he starts towards Beau, easily breaking my hold on the doorframe and pushing past me.

I race around the man, stalking towards my son, and put myself firmly between him and the psycho looking Santa Claus. I feel Beau's little hands grip onto the back of me, hindering my ability to move without trampling him.

Kris opens his arms wide like he wants to give Beau a hug, but he's still holding the knife. His Santa makeup is almost completely ruined after our struggle, and his stringy hair is hanging in his face so completely that I wonder how he can resist brushing it out of his eyes.

I stand in front of Beau, pushing him back, keeping him behind me, trying to make him move without taking my eyes off Kris. "Beau, go," I say, my voice low and urgent. "Go right now!" But he doesn't move out from behind me. I can feel his little body pressing up against mine, as if I can protect him from the horror standing in front of us. "Move!" I say louder, almost tripping over him as I try to take a step back.

The psycho Santa Claus takes a step closer. "And what would you like for Christmas this year, little boy?" he asks, his voice still that overly loud boom that he obviously thinks makes him sound like Santa Claus. I take a step back as Kris advances, still pushing my terrified son behind me. I look around, but there isn't an escape. Not with Beau frozen in terror. My heart is pounding in my ears. Any minute now, Kris will have us cornered. I have to do something.

"I hear you've been a good little boy," Kris says as he takes another step. I give Beau a firm push that sends him stumbling back, and leap at the crazy looking Santa Claus. "Beau, RUN!" I scream, grabbing the arm with the knife and shaking it violently. I'd hoped Kris would drop it, but no such luck. He reaches around, trying to grab the knife with his other hand, but I kick his arm away. Suddenly, he changes tactics, bringing the knife down, trying to stab me with it, but I've got both hands wrapped around his wrist. With a shriek of surprise, I'm pushed up against Kris' body as I fight to keep space between myself and the knife. Using his body as support, I'm finally able to stop the blade's momentum. It stops inches from my stomach. We stay there, me craddled up against his body, tucked into his armpit as if we're lovers, him trying to push the blade into me, me holding it away. It's as if we're in an arm wrestling match with two equally strong contestants.

He tries again to get the knife with his free hand, and I suddenly drop to the ground, twisting so the blade is no longer pointing towards me, trying to pull him down with me, but it's no use. He's too strong. Kris starts forward, dragging me along. He's moving towards Beau, who is still standing right where he landed when I pushed him earlier.

I'm dragged along helplessly, my body trailing behind me, both hands still wrapped around the wrist holding the knife. Kris stops and tries to shake me off, but I am not letting go. He turns towards me, and I pull my feet around and kick his feet out from under him. This time, he crashes to the floor, landing partly on top of me. Beau starts crying, little whimpers, but he still doesn't move.

Kris scrambles towards me, but I put my feet against him and, like a turtle on my back, slide across the hardwood floor. I keep the tension in my legs until Kris finally stops moving towards me. Scrambling, I roll over, crawl, then manage to get one foot, and then the other underneath me. I take a step towards my son, but a hand grabs my ankle and pulls me back. My legs fly out from underneath me. I hit the floor hard, but I don't feel the pain. I try again to motivate my son. "Beau! Go! Run!" I shout.

Suddenly, I'm being turned over onto my back and a warm body, Kris's, climbs on top of me. He straddles my waist and, instead of fighting him, I slap him hard across the face. It rings with a loud crack. Unfortunately, I don't react in time as he punches me back, hard, on the side of my face. Everything blurs as my limbs grow heavy. I sort of slump into the floor.

In a haze, I feel Kris crawl over and off of me, heading towards Beau. *Move!* I order my sluggish body. Somehow, I roll over in time to see Kris squatting down in front of my son. "And what do you want for Christmas this year, young man?" he booms. Beau is frozen, tears running down his face. "Get away from him!" I yell, forcing myself up and jumping on the man's back. I wrap my arms around Kris' neck and try to strangle him. I'm like a little monkey clinging to his back. He tries to shake me off, but I just hold on tighter, wrapping one arm around his neck and securing it with the other. *This is how you choke someone, right?*

Beau finally runs. Thank God! He runs into our bedroom and slams the door as Kris starts hitting me against the walls, hard, pounding my head and back again and again. I refuse to let go. Then he reaches up and grabs my face, trying to stick his thumb into my eye. I scream and let go of him, falling to the floor, hard. But I don't hesitate, I kick his legs out from under him, and he falls too.

I push myself up and try to run, but he grabs my ankles again, and again I fall, but this time I turn onto my back and start kicking him. "Get off me! Get off me!" I scream, kicking at him. I kick him in the face and get up again, running towards the front door. I pull it open and run outside. "Help!" I scream. "Help!"

11

HOLLY

I burst out of the house, my slippered feet slapping against the cold cement of my porch before I step out from under the stoop. Then it's the crunch of the snow as I pack it underfoot on the stairs. I cautiously race towards the police car parked in my driveway. It feels like it's miles away.

My breath comes in ragged gasps, the icy air burning my lungs while small puffs of steam hang in the air around my face. I'm moving as fast as I can, while being careful not to slip and fall down my cement front steps. I finally get to the bottom and then purposefully slide the short distance across my ice driveway to the cop car sitting there, silent and dark. I catch myself against the passenger door of the car.

"Help! Please! Help us!" I scream, pounding on the window. Even I can hear the terror in my voice. I glance back at the house and then do a double-take. Kris is standing on the porch, a stark red figure against a white backdrop. He starts down the stairs, slow, casual, as if he hasn't a care in the world.

I pound on the car window harder, desperate for a response, then peer into the dark interior. I can just make out the shape of a man sitting in the seat, his head slumped forward. *Is he asleep?* "Please!" I scream again, pounding harder, my fists aching. "Help us!"

I yank open the car door, and the officer's body slumps towards me, a dark, wet stain across his throat, soaking his uniform. Blood seeps from a jagged cut across his throat, dripping onto the officer's seat. My mind can't quite register what's happening fast enough as his head starts to slip off his body, falling towards me. I barely manage to move out of the way as it falls to the ground with a sickening thud. It rolls, leaving a trail of blood in the white snow, and my stomach heaves. His head stops moving, his lifeless eyes staring up at the night sky. I can't stop screaming as I get splattered with blood that's squirting out of the neck of the body still sitting in the passenger seat of the car.

My stomach lurching, I stumble back, recoiling from the gruesome sight, my hands flying to my mouth. I glance up at the driver's seat, and my eyes widen in fresh terror.

Officer Thistle, in the driver's seat, is tied and gagged. Her eyes are wide with fear, and she struggles against her bonds, her body shaking. She tries to speak through the kerchief tied across her mouth, but her muffled cries are unintelligible. I can barely look at her, my gaze drawn back to the bloody, headless body beside her, the horror of it making me want to vomit. I turn away, retching in the snow behind me, the bile burning my throat.

When I look up again, Kris is standing at the bottom of the stairs, watching me, his head tilted slightly, a disturbingly amused expression on his face.

Inside the car, Officer Thistle is desperately trying to get my attention, her eyes darting frantically between me and her partner's bloody body. She's trying to tell me something. Her muffled cries grow more frantic as I stand there dumbly, obviously not understanding what she wants. I look at the dead officer, wondering what she could possibly want me to do for him, then back at her, and she nods. She keeps saying something behind the gag over and over. *What is it?* My mind feels like it's underwater. Get the... Get the...GUN! Like a lightning bolt, it hits me. His gun. She's telling me to get his gun.

I glance back at Officer Thistle, understanding dawning, but I hesitate. Her partner's head is lying at my feet between me and his body, a gruesome obstacle. It's as if the head is saying that I am not to go anywhere near his gun. But *why not?* I ask the head at my feet. *You won't be needing it.* I stifle a hysterical giggle. *Jokes? Now? Really?* It occurs to me I could be going into shock, and I shake myself. Now is not the time.

Officer Thistle's muffled screams intensify, urging me to hurry, her eyes filled with terror. I lick my lips, my mouth suddenly dry, and try not to look down as I force myself to step over the head, moving towards the open car door and the headless body inside.

The smell of blood is thick in the air, making me gag. My hand trembles as I reach for the gun. It's slick with the officer's blood, the cold, sticky liquid coating my fingers. I recoil instinctively, wiping my hand on my pajamas, then take a deep breath, forcing myself to grasp it firmly. I try to pull it from the holster, but it's stuck. I tug harder, shaking it, but it won't budge.

Suddenly, Officer Thistle stiffens, her eyes widening in terror.

"He was naughty."

My shoulders hunch at the feel of his breath on my neck. "It's Santaaaa..." he sings softly, announcing himself with the enthusiastic introduction.

I whirl around, my heart leaping into my throat. Kris looms over me, way inside my personal bubble. I back up against the side of the police car, pressing myself against the bloody corpse. It's preferable to the Santa standing much too close, straddling the bloody head with his feet.

The cold seeps through my thin pajamas, and it's hard to know if I'm trembling out of fear or because I'm slowly freezing.

"How can cops be naughty?" I ask, my voice trembling, trying to buy myself time. My fingers fumble with the holster behind me. "They literally swear an oath to serve and protect."

With a snap, the holster finally unclasps. My shoulders slump in relief as I awkwardly grasp the gun and pull.

"They took my Daddy away on Christmas Day," Kris says, his voice rising, becoming more agitated. His eyes fill with a dark, burning rage.

"He murdered your mother," I say, my voice firm, trying to keep him talking, trying to distract him from my frantic fumbling.

"He *had* to!" Kris screams, his voice cracking, the memory clearly causing him immense pain. "She was naughty!" He says, his voice full of venom.

With another pull, I finally manage to free the gun from its holster. I turn it in my hands behind me, trying to figure out how to palm it correctly. My hands are shaking uncontrollably, but I feel my palm wrap around the handle, and my finger come to rest on the trigger. Feeling triumphant, I raise the gun and point it at Kris. He looks down with surprise but seems unconcerned. He barely pulls away from me, as if waiting to see what I will do, but I'm not hesitating. The head at my feet has me motivated to put an end to this nightmare right now. I pull on the trigger, waiting for the kick, but nothing happens.

"It stuck!" I shout, my statement a desperate request for help.

Officer Thistle, still tied and gagged in the car, starts shouting around the gag, her muffled cries sounding desperate, trying to tell me something.

I look down at the gun, confused.

Kris bursts into laughter, a high-pitched, manic sound.

Wait! The safety would be on. I frantically begin to search for the little switch that will let me fire the gun, but Kris backhands me across the face, sending me crashing into the car beside me and then to the ground.

Pain explodes in my head, my vision blurring as I hit the concrete. But I don't let go of the gun. I lay there cradling it until I feel a foot kick me in the stomach. Pain explodes inside me, and I curl up on myself as Kris' boot kicks me again and again. I let out a small sob, the pain shooting through my ribs. I have to move, but he's standing over me, his hands braced against the car as he kicks me. There's only one way out of this. I uncurl and roll onto my back, then scooch under the car, out of his reach.

Kris saunters around the vehicle, his heavy boots crunching on the snow. "Here comes Sant-a, here comes Sant-a..." he sings, his voice sending shivers down my spine.

Cold and wet seeps into my pajamas, freezing me even as the snow melts underneath me. I lay on my back under the car, watching Kris' boots as he saunters around to the front of the vehicle.

Suddenly, he drops to his knees, peering under the car. I shriek, scrambling backwards, pointing the gun at him with trembling hands. He waggles a finger at me, his eyes glinting in the darkness.

"Uh, uh, uh," he says, his voice a mocking whisper. "I see you..." He sings-songs.

Focus Holly! I force myself to ignore him and focus on the gun in my hand. *Where is the...?* I flip a little switch near the grip with a click! Kris continues his walk around the car, singing to himself. I hear the car door open and Officer Thistle's muffled screams as she's pulled from the vehicle.

Shit!

I listen, my heart pounding in my chest as he drags her back around the vehicle towards me. I start to push out from under the car, but I'm confronted by Officer Pine's head, lying on the ground, his dead eyes staring at me, his blood soaking red into the snow. I freeze, my stomach churning.

Officer Thistle screams again, her cries muffled by the gag, a sound of pure terror. It takes all my willpower to force myself towards the severed head and out from under the car.

I kneel in the snow, the ice and concrete hard beneath my knees, my whole body shaking. I'm not sure if it's from terror or the cold. I have to hold the gun in front of me with both hands to keep it steady.

Kris is standing with Officer Thistle in front of him, using her as a human shield, his knife pressed against her throat, the blade glinting in the moonlight.

I freeze, my heart sinking. I concentrate on keeping the gun steady, but my hands won't stop trembling.

"So naughty," Kris says, his eyes fixed on me, a disappointed smile twisting his painted lips.

"Let her go," I say, my voice trembling but firm.

He shakes his head, his eyes glinting with a manic intensity.

He pushes the knife deeper into Officer Thistle's throat, and she gasps in pain, her muffled cries intensifying.

"Okay, okay," I say quickly, my voice pleading. "Just don't hurt her. She's... she's good, remember? She's nice."

I slowly lower the gun towards the ground, my heart sinking with each inch. But just as I set it down, Officer Thistle, in a desperate act of bravery, suddenly headbutts Kris in the face.

Kris screams, his head rearing back. He lets go of Officer Thistle, and she stumbles forward, running towards me. I scramble to retrieve the gun from the ground.

"Come on!" I yell to Thistle, urging her to hurry, but just as she reaches me, BANG!

Officer Thistle jerks, then stumbles to a halt. She looks down at her chest, her eyes widening in disbelief. I follow her gaze and see the dark red stain blooming across her uniform.

"Nooo!" I scream in horror as Kris laughs, a chilling, triumphant sound. He waves the gun he took from Thistle's belt in the air. "She. Was. Naughtyyyy," he sings the last word, while shaking the gun at her like a normal person would waggle a finger.

I point my gun at Kris and pull the trigger. This time it fires. His leg flies out from underneath him, and he hits the ground hard. He grabs his leg, screaming in pain. I've hit him. It's a Christmas miracle.

Officer Thistle stumbles and falls to the ground, grasping onto me to slow her fall. Blood spews from her mouth, hitting me in the face as I try to catch her. I recoil, then recover, pressing my shaking hand against her chest, trying to stop the bleeding. But it's no use. The blood keeps flowing.

"I'm so sorry," I whisper, tears streaming down my face.

Officer Thistle stares at me, her eyes wide and unseeing.

Suddenly, bullets slam into the police car behind me, the metal pinging and shattering. Kris is firing his gun, his manic laughter echoing through the night. I flinch and scream as the shots ring out, the sound deafening.

I jump to my feet and run, making a desperate break for the house. Bullets fly past me as I race up the front steps and burst in through the front door. I slam the door shut behind me and quickly turn the lock. I pause for a moment, catching my breath, then run towards the back door, checking the lock there too.

"Barry? Beau? Beau!" I call out, my voice strained.

I run to the kitchen sink and frantically wash the blood off the gun, then wipe Officer Thistle's blood off my face with the back of my hand, unknowingly smearing it.

I start to search through the house, my eyes darting around the rooms. "My phone. My phone," I mutter to myself. "Where is my phone?" I scream louder, my voice echoing through the empty house. Frantically, I search the living room, checking the coffee table, the couch, the chairs. Then I rush into the kitchen.

Beau suddenly appears, clutching a cell phone in his hand.

"Beau! Good boy!" I say, relief washing over me as I rush towards him. Falling to my knees, I pull him into a tight hug, then quickly check him over. He seems unharmed. *My poor boy! He is gonna need so much therapy after this.* "Are you okay?" I ask. But I don't wait for an answer. There isn't time.

Still holding the gun in one hand, I grab the phone from him and dial 911. It rings. "Is Daddy okay?" I ask Beau, my voice trembling, as I wait for someone to answer.

Suddenly, a window breaks, the sound of shattering glass making us both jump. I leap to my feet and start pushing Beau in front of me. "Upstairs!" I say, my voice urgent. "Go!"

I drop the phone, holding the gun with two shaky hands, and pointing it in the direction of where the sound of someone breaking one of our windows had come from. "Move!" I urge him.

This time, he obeys, dashing up the stairs. I follow right behind him, keeping the gun raised.

The 911 operator's voice comes from the phone lying uselessly on the floor. "911 operator. What's your emergency?"

12
HOLLY

I race up the stairs, helping Beau as he stumbles. We stop at the top, unsure of where to go next. The hallway yawns open in front of us, with several doors to choose from. *Which one?* I start down the hall, pushing Beau in front of me, considering the different doors. Bathroom, linen closet, office, guest bedroom. I decide on the last one. I yank open the door to the guest bedroom and hurry Beau inside, then across the room to the closet. I open the closet door. It's mostly empty. I only use it for storage, so there is plenty of room in there, but nothing extra to hide him, but it'll have to do.

"Okay," I whisper, crouching down so we are eye to eye. "I have to go get daddy. Lock this door behind me, then get in the closet and shut the door, okay? I'll be right back."

I turn to leave, but Beau grabs my arm. "Don't leave!"

I stop and hug him tight. "Honey, I'm sorry, but you need to be super brave," I whisper, kissing his forehead. "I have to go help daddy."

"You don't," Beau says, shaking his head, tears in his eyes. "I untied him."

"You did?" I ask, surprised. "Did he wake up?"

"He moved," Beau says. "I splashed water in his face."

Relief floods through me. "Good job, baby!" I whisper. "Okay, you stay here. I'll be right back."

"No! Stay with me," Beau pleads.

I gently but firmly pull his hands away from me. "Beau! I'll be right back," I repeat.

Beau cries as I get up and quietly open the bedroom door. I peek out into the hallway. It's all clear. I turn back to Beau. "Lock this door and don't open it for anyone but me," I say.

Beau, still crying, nods. I take a deep breath and step out into the hallway. The latch clicks behind me as he locks the door.

Gun in hand, I creep along the hallway, staying close to the wall, out of the light. My breathing is fast and uneven.

I stop at the top of the stairs and look down into the kitchen and living room. They are both empty.

The phone at the bottom of the stairs beeps loudly. I swallow hard and tiptoe down the stairs, cringing at every creak. *I need that phone.*

I step down off the last step, looking around wildly. Nothing. *Where is he?*

Carefully, watching, I crouch down and reach for the phone. My fingertips brush it... I almost have it when a bloody foot steps from around the corner and onto the phone, crushing it.

I fall back onto my butt, then bring the gun out in front of me. Kris grins down at me, shaking his head. "Uh, uh, uh," he says.

Blood drips down his leg, soaking the top of his shoe. *He knows I'll shoot him, right?* I mean, I've done it before.

"Merry Christmas, asshole!" I yell, about to pull the trigger, when Barry suddenly steps around the corner, swinging a hammer at Kris's head.

I quickly point the gun at the ceiling, away from both of them, as Barry swings the hammer I keep in our closet for hanging pictures at Kris's head. Kris leaps back, dodging. Barry swings again and again, moving towards Kris, trying to hit him, but Kris manages to dodge and get out of the way every time.

Barry swings again, but instead of backing away from the swing, Kris leaps at Barry, grabbing his arm and pulling him close. Kris grabs the hammer, trying to wrestle it away, but Barry is putting up a fight.

I watch in agony, unable to help, as I point my gun at the two of them. I don't dare shoot. I could hit my husband. Suddenly, Kris lets go of the hammer and pushes Barry away. Unprepared for the sudden release and change in momentum, Barry stumbles back, then tries to regain his footing. He's just straightening up when Kris nonchalantly raises his gun and shoots him.

Barry screams as the bullet penetrates his flesh, hitting him in the shoulder. The force of it backs him up against the wall. The hammer falls harmlessly to the floor with a loud metallic thud. Barry grabs the wall to steady himself with one bloody hand and then slides down the wall to the floor, leaving a long bloody handprint behind him.

"NO!" I scream, angry at myself for hesitating to shoot this asshole. I point the gun at Kris and fire, but Kris drops to the floor next to Barry.

"Shoot him! Holly, shoot him!" Barry yells.

But Kris grabs Barry and pulls him in front of him, on top of him, like a shield. Kris starts to laugh as Barry tries to get away.

I stand up and calmly walk towards the two men. *I have him now.* Barry is trying to get away from Kris, but Kris has him around the waist, keeping him between himself and me.

"Yeah. That's not gonna work, idiot," I say, pointing the gun right at Kris's head, almost touching his forehead with it.

I am about to pull the trigger when Kris grabs one of my ankles and pulls hard.

I fly backward, landing hard on the hardwood floor. I lose my grip on the gun, and it clatters loudly as it skids across the floor. For a moment, I can't get any air into my lungs, and I lie there gasping. I can't quite recover until, painfully slowly, air makes its way back into my body. I push myself upright, feeling like someone just ran me over.

Barry and Kris are still on their backs, Barry on top, struggling to get free of Kris's hold around his waist. Kris is laughing gleefully, like they are two pals having a little fun. Barry snaps his elbow back into Kris's face, and Kris's head hits the floor with a loud thud. Kris' arms loosen, and Barry, finally free, rolls over. Straddling Kris, he punches him hard in the face, but Kris just laughs.

"Get the fuck away from my family!" Barry yells, punching him again and again, but he can only use one arm; the other one hangs uselessly at his side.

I push myself up. No time for whining. "Barry!" I yell, and I hurry towards the two fighting men.

"Go get Beau," Barry says over his shoulder, then goes back to punching Kris in the face. But Kris is still laughing. *Gees! What is with this guy?*

I hesitate. What should I do? *Should I go get Beau?* That seems like a bad idea, with Barry shot and Kris still laughing like a lunatic.

I hesitate, frozen with uncertainty, then get an idea.

I run into the bedroom and grab the rope that Kris had used to tie Barry. Triumphant, I try to run from the room only to be yanked almost off my feet. The rope is still tied to the chair. *No!* I run to the chair, frantically tugging on the rope, trying to untie it. "Come on! Come on!" I say, tugging at the rope, wasting time in my haste to get it free. I can hear the men still fighting. I force myself to slow down and focus, methodically untying the knots that are keeping the rope attached to the chair. Finally, it comes free. I breathe a sigh of relief and run back into the living room carrying my prize, but Barry is lying face down on the floor, and Kris is gone.

FUCK!

I rush to Barry's side. "Barry?"

I turn him over. His nose is bleeding. His head lolls to one side, making my heart sink into my stomach. *NO!* "Barry? No!"

I put my ear to his chest, listening for his heartbeat. I sigh in relief when I hear it. *Thank you, God!* I put my hands over his bullet wound and try to stop the bleeding.

I suddenly feel very exposed. *Where is Kris?*

I need my... I look around the room, then start searching more frantically. *Where are they?* "The guns," I whisper. "No. No. NO! The guns! Idiot!" I hit myself on the forehead with the heels of my hands in disbelief. "Always take the guns!"

I see the phone on the floor and crawl to it, but it's broken. I throw it down, swearing. "Dammit!" I look around the quiet house and then see the hammer. Crawling towards it, I grab the handle. My hands are covered in Barry's blood, making them slide along the smooth wood, but it's better than nothing.

Is it? A small voice inside me whispers. *What good is a hammer against guns?*

Just then, the doorbell rings. I freeze. Still kneeling on the floor, holding the hammer, I look at the front door. Someone knocks.

Slowly, I get to my feet. I look around the room, then at the door. Someone knocks again.

I walk to the door and look through the small window. Rudy Frost, our neighbor, is standing on the porch, trying to see inside.

He is about to knock again when I call out through the door. "Rudy? Go home! Call the police!"

"Holly? Is everything okay in there?" Rudy asks. "We heard shots."

"Go home and call the police!" I repeat with urgency.

"Mary is calling the police... Let me in. Is everyone okay?" Rudy asks.

I look at Barry on the floor, think for a moment, and then yank the door open.

Rudy's eyes widen as he takes in my appearance, my face, hands, and clothes covered in blood, the hammer in my hands, and then he sees Barry. His mouth falls open.

"What the hell?" he says. He glances toward the bloody hammer in my hand. I shut the front door, then run to Barry. Dropping the hammer, I grab Barry by the arms and lift him up.

"Rudy. Help me," I say. "Help me get him out of here."

13
DETECTIVE DONNOR

I stare at the macabre pictures until my eyes ache. Eleven days. Eleven bodies. Eleven young women, each found beneath a Christmas tree, their throats meticulously cut, their bodies dressed and arranged like human dolls.

The Kris Kringle Killer. The nickname repeats over and over in my brain. It's catchy. We'd unfortunately been unable to stop the press from giving him the catchy little nickname. We'd tried. The name made him sound cute and unthreatening. If only the press understood how much damage they do in cases like these, glorifying monsters and both scaring people and diminishing the threat.

The thought is interrupted by Cane and Wiseman getting back to the precinct. I hear them come in and stand, eager to get my hands on the lab results they should be carrying, but when I get to them, they are empty-handed.

"Where are the results?" I ask, looking back and forth between them, impatient for an answer.

"We don't have the results," Wiseman says, as if that should be obvious.

"Why not?" I ask, unable to keep the edge out of my voice.

"Chief!" Cane says, placatingly. "John pulled the prints, but he has to run them through the system. You know how long it takes. He said he'd call us if anything pops."

If anything pops? The thought makes me tired. *What if nothing pops?* "Did you tell him to start by comparing them to the prints we have on file for Kris Connors?" I ask.

"Yes, Chief. We told him to start there," Wiseman answers, obviously annoyed that I am questioning their competency, but I don't care. If we were better... If we'd done better, eleven women wouldn't be dead, and Holly wouldn't have been attacked tonight.... Wouldn't still be in danger.

The thought reminds me. "You two head up to the Woods' house. I want you there as backup for Thistle and Pine."

Wiseman and Cane look at each other, surprised. Cane apparently loses whatever silent conversation passes between them because he speaks. "You're sure?" He asks. "If our guy decides to attack someone else, we'll all be stuck up in the mountains in that snow. Our response time will be..." I see him wanting to say something honest, like 'horrendous' or 'extremely poor'. Instead, he finishes with "'bad."

They're right. If I'm wrong and Kris isn't focused on Holly, we should have at least one unit here to respond to calls. But I can't shake the feeling in my gut. I sigh and run a hand through my already messy hair. *Why didn't I retire last year when I had the chance?* I could be at home right now, surrounded by the warmth of my family, the scent of pine needles and cinnamon in the air, watching an old Christmas movie. Now this holiday, this Christmas, would haunt me forever.

The weight of responsibility presses down on me, a suffocating blanket. These girls, they'd been daughters, sisters, friends. Their families probably weren't celebrating at all. Christmas would never be the same for any of them. And I was supposed to be bringing them some semblance of justice. I was doing a piss poor job of it, but then, how do you catch someone who doesn't act like a rational human being?

I make a decision. "You two go. I'll stay here and wait for the lab results. I'll also respond to any calls that come in. I want you two up on that mountain." I look between the two officers and realize they agree with the decision. They were just doing their job of making sure they were in the best possible place.

"Sure thing, Chief," Cane responds. "Let me just use the little boy's room, and we'll be on our way."

"I'm gonna grab a coffee. You want some?" Wiseman asks Cane, the two of them already in motion.

"Yes, please. I have a thermos on my desk."

"I'll grab it," Wiseman tells him, and the two of them leave me standing there with nothing to do but go back to my desk and continue to confront my own failure. My shoulders droop a little bit, but I feel good about the decision to send them to the Woods' house. My gut tells me it's the right call.

I turn and walk back into my office, but I can't take any more of the pictures. I close the files and then stretch, putting both feet up on my desk and leaning back in my chair. I close my eyes and let out a long sigh. Nothing to do but wait until results come in or someone calls. *Please, God, don't let anyone call.* It feels like every call lately is some catastrophe. I keep my eyes shut, not allowing myself to look at the phone. I may have to throw this phone away. It feels... tainted.

I can hear Cane and Wiseman getting ready to leave, lingering in the warmth for a little longer than absolutely necessary on their way out. I feel my body relax. *What time is it?* It's definitely somewhere in the middle of the night. I can feel myself drifting. Sleep wouldn't be such a bad thing. It feels like I haven't slept in ages. Just as my head begins to nod, the office door flies open. Officer Cane stands in the doorway, his face pale, his eyes wide with a mixture of urgency and dread. My eyes snap open, adrenaline surging through my veins. "Yeah?" I bark, my voice rough with fatigue.

"We just got word that a 911 call came from the Woods' house about ten minutes ago, but when the 911 operator answered, no one was on the line," Cane says, his voice tight. "Now, the neighbors next door are calling about shots being fired. They said it sounded like the shots came from the direction of the Woods' home."

I stand up, the chair scraping against the linoleum floor. "Have you heard from our unit there?" I ask, my voice sharp.

"No," Cane replies, his voice laced with apprehension. "We can't reach them. We're heading there now."

A curse escapes my lips. "Get as many officers there as fast as you can," I order, my voice ringing with urgency. "Do we have anyone close by?"

"No," Cane says, his voice heavy. "Everyone's off. It's Christmas Eve."

"Fucking holidays!" I spit, the words laced with bitterness. I grab my jacket, the waterproof material cold against my skin. "Let's go."

We rush out of the office, grabbing Wiseman as we go, the urgency of the situation propelling us forward. Our squad cars are parked near the entrance. Wiseman and Cane jump into their vehicle, and I into mine. I reach into my jacket pocket looking for my keys, but find none. I search my other pocket and then my pants.

"Dammit!" I swear, hitting the steering wheel. I open my door and jump out of my shop. Cane and Wiseman have already pulled out of their spot, their red and blue lights flashing against the darkness. I walk towards them, and Wiseman rolls down his window.

"I forgot my keys," I say, feeling like a foolish old man who shouldn't be in charge of a murder investigation. "You two go ahead. I'm right behind you." They pull out as I race back to the precinct and shove open the door. Warmth and silence surround me. One of the lights overhead buzzes to life, activated by my sudden presence. I'm heading to my office when my phone rings. The noise makes me jump. *Jesus, what is wrong with me tonight?* I look at the caller ID. It's my wife. I answer it as I walk down the hall.

"Hi, honey," I say. "What are you still doing up?"

"Where are you?" My wife's voice is laced with anger and impatience.

"Working," I say defensively.

"It's Christmas Eve," She informs me as if I am not aware.

"Honey, I am a cop, and there is a serial killer on the loose." I get to my office and start searching through the papers on my desk for my keys.

"And none of the other cops have taken the night off?" She asks.

I continue looking for my keys, both distracted and choosing not to answer. "It's the middle of the night. You have to sleep," she continues, firm but gentle this time. "You can't do more than you can do."

I bite my lip on a retort. *I should be doing more... But what?* Instead, I say, "Honey, I have to go. Go to sleep. I'll be there in the morning." And God, I hope that's true, that I'll be snuggled in bed next to my wife and not at a house where another murdered young woman sits beneath a Christmas tree. I move the file containing all the photos of the murdered "dolls" and finally find my keys. I snatch them up, not paying attention to what my wife is saying, although I do register the concern in her voice.

"Honey," I interrupt her. "I have to go. I'll call you later." I hang up the phone with an inward cringe. I'm gonna pay for that later.

I'm already moving back down the hall. Again, I shove open the front door, but this time an icy breeze hits me full in the face. My breath fogs as I pull my jacket up around my neck to keep the cold away. I put the key in the keyhole and turn it. This time, the engine roars to life, the sound a defiant growl against the night's stillness. I slam the car into reverse, tires crunching on the snow, and back out of the parking spot.

I hit the gas, the car lurching forward, and speed away from the precinct, my flashing lights cutting through the darkness like a beacon. The streets are deserted, the houses dark and silent, their festive decorations a mocking reminder of the holiday cheer that was murdered this season.

The silence is broken only by the wail of the sirens and the rhythmic thump of the windshield wipers. I grip the steering wheel, my knuckles white, my mind racing. *Please, God, let her be okay.* I'm not sure I can take it if we are waiting at the house for the guy and his target still gets murdered.

Houses blur past, and streetlights become a flickering ribbon of light. I push my speed to the limit. It's still slower than I want to go, but ending up in a snow drift won't help anybody. The ominous feeling that we're too late steals over my whole body. "Please!" I say it out loud this time. "Don't let us be too late this time." The image of the girls, their lifeless bodies arranged beneath the Christmas trees, flashes through my mind. *Not this time,* I think to myself. *Not this time.*

14
HOLLY

Barry is starting to get heavy, and I haven't even lifted him yet. I stand there, Barry's arms in my hands, waiting for Rudy to pick up his legs. Rudy hurries to my side, his eyes wide as he stares at Barry's limp body. I struggle to lift him, my arms shaking with the effort. Rudy's mouth hangs open. "I can't believe you actually did it," he says, his voice a low, disbelieving murmur.

Using his arms, I start pulling Barry towards the door. His weight is dead and heavy. "Get his feet," I tell Rudy, my voice strained, my mind going a million miles per second.

Rudy just stands there. "I don't think you should move him."

I ignore him and keep dragging Barry. He moans softly, a low, painful sound stabbing straight into me.

"Holly, you're hurting him!" Rudy says, his voice rising in alarm.

"Rudy, help me get him out of here," I repeat, my voice desperate. "The killer is still in the house, and I have to go get Beau."

But Rudy doesn't budge. "Where do you think we're gonna take him?"

I think. *Where can we take him?* Where would be safe? "To your house," I decide. "Now get his legs," I snap.

Rudy pulls out a phone. "You're not pinning this on me," he says, his eyes shifting nervously.

"Oh, thank God. A phone," I breathe, relief washing over me. I rush to grab Rudy's phone out of his hands, but Rudy pulls it out of reach.

"Rudy!" I say, impatiently.

Suddenly, we hear a noise from upstairs – a creak, a muffled thump.

Beau!

"Stay here with Barry," I tell Rudy, grabbing the hammer. Barry flinches away from me, but my mind doesn't process what that means. I shove the hammer into his hands. "I have to get Beau. I'll be right back."

I turn to leave, but Rudy grabs my arm. I look at him, surprised.

"Holly... Look," Rudy says, his voice low and urgent. "We still have time before the police get here." I stare at him, waiting.

"I can help get you out of this," Rudy continues. "I'll say that I heard Barry threatening you. That he found out about your... affair, and he attacked you. I got here just in time to see you defend yourself..."

My mouth hangs open as I wait for what he's said to make sense but then lose patience. "What are you talking about?" I ask, completely confused, my mind on my son upstairs.

"I'm saying I can be persuaded..." Rudy says, his grip tightening on my arm. "If you need me to cover for you with the cops... All I'd need is a little... Persuading... Maybe some of what you're giving to your... Paramour..." He looks at me in a way that disgusts me, a slimy, knowing look that makes me want to crawl out of my skin. I jerk my arm out of his grasp.

"Excuse me?" I say, my voice cold and hard, then it dawns on me what he's just said.

"Why does everyone think I am cheating on Barry?" I ask, baffled.

I turn to head up the stairs, but he grabs my arm again. "Look, I'm not asking for much," he says. "Just every now and then... Surely that's not too much to ask for helping you get out of this." He gestures toward Barry.

"Out of what?" I ask.

"Murdering Barry!" he says.

"I did not murder Barry!" I say so angrily that Rudy takes a step back.

"Look, I get it," Rudy says. "Divorce is messy. Splitting money... Custody battles... This is just... easier." He says it in a way that makes murdering your spouse seem like the only obvious option. I can't help my expression as I stare at Rudy. I've lived next to this guy for seventeen years. *What the hell?*

I jerk my arm away from him for the second time. "You are an idiot," I hiss.

I start up the stairs. He follows me a step. "I'm guessing Barry found out..." he says.

I round on him. "There's nothing for Barry to find out about, and I didn't do this," I say.

Rudy thinks for a second, and a stubborn look tilts his chin. "That's not what I'll tell people," he says.

For the first time, I stop and really face him, my jaw tight. "Rudy, I was attacked earlier tonight by the Kris Kringle Killer," I say. "The cops know all about it. In fact, they're parked right outside. Did you not see the dead bodies?"

Rudy's head turns toward where I am pointing, but the walls block his view of the street. "What dead bodies? I came through the yard," he says.

"This..." I say, gesturing between the two of us, "will never happen. Now, watch Barry while I go get Beau!" I start up the stairs again. There isn't time for this.

"Look, you should at least consider..." Rudy says.

I don't even look back. "Rudy," I call over my shoulder, "if that psychopath has Beau, I'm going to beat the shit out of you with that hammer."

Rudy watches me go, looking defeated. He looks down at Barry's unconscious body. "Poor bastard," he mutters.

Rudy kneels by Barry and slaps his cheeks a few times. "Barry. Barry! Time to wake up and realise your wife has tried to kill you," he says. Barry's eyes flutter.

Upstairs, I creep towards the guest bedroom door. I stop, very aware of the other dark doorways around me. I take a deep breath and try the doorknob. It's locked.

I knock softly. "Beau? Beau? Can you hear me?" I listen but hear nothing. I knock again. "Baby, I need you to open the door."

I hear movement inside, and the door opens a crack. I peek in and then crouch down. "Hi," I whisper to Beau.

15
KRIS

The stone is frozen and covered in bits of ice and snow. It cuts into my fingers as I climb up the outside of the house, pulling myself up the brick wall with my fingernails. My hands feel like they are being sliced by a thousand tiny cuts. It feels... Interesting.

Silently, I slide the window open and climb inside. I've already climbed through this window once tonight. I giggle. I like to be someplace surprising. If I came down the chimney, they might be expecting me, but a window? No. It's more fun.

I climb into the room and look around for the second time tonight. This used to be my room when I was little, but it doesn't look like my room anymore. All of my toys are gone, along with my bed and the little desk where Mom and I worked on my numbers and colored together. Instead, there is a large bed with a sky-blue comforter and lots of throw pillows. Two bedside tables with lamps and a love seat against one wall. A tall dresser is the last of the room's furniture. This time, I open one of the dresser drawers, but there's nothing inside it. I frown, perplexed. I don't think anyone sleeps here.

I shake off the melancholy feeling the room gives me and start toward the door. I'm about to sneak out into the hallway when suddenly I hear a sound. Someone is crying. Concern wrinkles my brow. *Who could be crying tonight?* It's Christmas Eve. Santa is here.

I walk towards the sound, stopping in front of my old closet. I slowly open the door and find myself huddled on the floor. The little boy's eyes widen in fear when he sees me, and he starts trembling. I crouch down in front of him. "You don't have to be scared," I tell him. "Daddy isn't here." I smile at the thought. *We're safe. Daddy isn't here.*

The little boy doesn't answer, just stares at me with those wide, fearful eyes. I recognize the fear in his eyes, a reflection of my own. The interior of the closet feels so familiar... Safe. It was where I usually went when Mommy told me to "Go. Hide."

I suddenly realize that that was probably why Dad always found me. The thought bothers me, and I frown.

The little boy starts crying, so I crawl into the closet with him and sit down. "It's okay," I say softly. "Santa's here." I reach out a hand, my fingers brushing against his cheek. He flinches, crying harder.

"Nice," I say softly, my voice soothing. "Nice." I smile, but he cringes away from me, tears rolling down his cheeks. *What is wrong with this kid? Doesn't he know I'm Santa Claus?* My eyes widen. *No! No! No!*

I suddenly know what's wrong. Even though it's dark inside the closet, the boy can see me. My hair has fallen into my face and looks dirty and scraggly. My white beard is around my neck, and my makeup is smeared. It's all wrong. So wrong! I hurriedly fix my beard, pulling it up onto my face where it belongs. *Sloppy. Sloppy! Dad would be so disappointed.*

"I'm reading my list. Checking it twice," I say, my voice a low whisper. "I already know who's naughty or nice." I try to make it sound reassuring, but he just keeps crying as he squirms back, away from me. I bite my lip, trying to think of a way to comfort him.

The small, cramped space is warm with just enough light filtering through the slightly open closet door. It feels nice to be safe... Even though we aren't safe. Daddy will find us. He always does. We sit in silence for a moment, listening to the sounds of the house. I frown in displeasure. Someone new is in the house. *Shouldn't all the good boys and girls be asleep? Whoever it is, they must be naughty.*

I hear the newcomer argue with Mom... no, Holly. Holly sounds angry. She threatens to beat the person with a hammer and then... Another pause. I listen as someone starts opening the kitchen drawers, opening and closing them with a clatter, searching for something.

I hear Holly's husband say something that sounds like..." Not safe?" he repeats it, his voice weak. Yes. That's what he said. "It's not safe. Get them out."

"Don't worry," the newcomer says, his voice low. "The police are on their way. They'll lock up your wife for good for this."

I turn to the boy next to me. The one so much like me. "Mom has been naughty," I tell him, my voice a low whisper.

He shakes his head, his eyes wide with terror.

"I know," I say softly, understanding his terror and sadness. It makes me sad, too. "I saw mommy...." I look at him, a sad glint in my eye. "She's on the naughty list. So we have to...."

The boy shrinks back further into the corner, trembling with fear. I reach out and gently stroke his hair.

"Don't worry," I whisper. "I'll do it. You don't have to."

I feel tears prick my eyes as I think about what I have to do. *It's her fault. She put herself on the naughty list.* But it still makes me sad. At least it will be better without all the blood...

Careful not to mess up my makeup, I wipe my tears and reach for the rope in my pocket.

16
HOLLY

I peer into Beau's eyes as he stands at the door, his lower lip trembles, and he starts to cry, his little face crumpling with fear. My heart breaks, and guilt wrenches me in two. I can't believe this is happening to my son, and I can't even protect him. "Shh," I whisper. "It's okay... Mr. Frost is here," I say, trying to sound reassuring, but I can't help the quiver in my voice.

My brow furrows as I suddenly notice something white wrapped around Beau's neck. I reach towards him, a shiver of fear coursing through me.

"Beau?" I whisper, my voice barely a breath. "What's...?"

The door is suddenly flung open wide.

Kris is standing behind Beau. I gasp, recoiling in horror. Beau starts to cry in earnest, his small body shaking as he is suddenly yanked back by the thin rope around his neck.

I move towards my son, my heart pounding in my chest. "Stop it! Stop it!" I command, but I stop abruptly as the rope is pulled tighter, jerking Beau upright. The rope cuts off his cries, leaving only a small, choked gasp.

"Uh, uh, uh," Kris whispers, his painted red lips curving into a chilling smile.

"I will kill you!" I scream, my voice raw with terror and rage. Tears prick my eyes, and a helplessness I've never experienced before overwhelms me.

Kris holds the ends of the rope, the rough fibers digging into Beau's delicate skin. Hot, wet tears stream down Beau's face, mixing with the streaks of dirt and fear. My fury gives way to fear, and I will do anything, *anything*, to make this stop happening to Beau.

I hear Barry's voice coming from downstairs, weak but insistent. "Help her. Help her!" *Barry! Help me!*

I hear Rudy answer, "Alright," "But you're a better man than I am…"

Hurry! I think as I watch Beau's face turn blue.

"Please," I whisper, and it seems to reach Kris, who suddenly realizes that he needs to let Beau breathe. He loosens the rope a touch, and Beau gulps in mouthfuls of air.

Rudy starts up the stairs, his footsteps slow and hesitant. Barry calls after him, his voice weak but urgent. "Rudy." Rudy's footsteps stop, and I scream at him in my mind to *hurry! Why would Barry stop him?*

I hear something heavy and metallic scrape across the floor, and then Barry says, "Here. Hurry!"

The hammer. Good thinking, Barry!

"Back!" Kris orders me, and I immediately take a step back, willing to obey his every request if he will just stop hurting Beau. I wait for Kris to follow before taking another one, keeping the distance between Beau and me relatively close.

Rudy's nonchalant footsteps echo through the house, and then Rudy, himself, finally appears at the top of the stairs. His eyes widen at the scene in front of him. Kris, with his clown-like Santa makeup, is holding Beau by the rope around his neck. I stand across from them, my body tense, ready.

Rudy looks between us, his face pale. "What the hell?"

"Mr. Frost, is it?" Kris says, his voice smooth and chilling. "Shouldn't you be in bed. What will Santa think?" he asks softly, the words dripping with menace.

Rudy doesn't move, his eyes fixed on the rope around Beau's neck.

Kris gives a small, sharp tug on the rope, and Beau cries out in pain as he stumbles back. I cry out too, my hands clenching into fists, but I don't dare do more than that.

Rudy puts a hand out, as if trying to calm Kris, but sweat is beading on his forehead. "Okay, let's... Stay calm... Nobody needs to get hurt," he stammers, his voice trembling.

Kris starts to laugh, a high-pitched, manic sound that echoes through the house.

"Give me the hammer," I say to Rudy, my voice low and urgent.

He doesn't move, his eyes wide with terror.

"Then hit him! What are you waiting for?" I yell.

Rudy stares blankly between Kris and me, then seems to finally realize he's holding a hammer. He tightens his grip on it, and for the first time, looks like he might actually use it. "Let the boy go," he says, his voice shaking.

Kris looks thoughtful for a moment, then raises his other arm high, a knife glinting in his hand. "I don't think I will," he says, his voice a chilling whisper.

He brings the knife down towards Beau's chest.

"No!" I scream, leaping at Kris and grabbing his arm with all my strength.

"Son of a..." Kris yells, the force of my jump throwing him off balance. He lets go of the rope around Beau's neck.

I hang on Kris's arm with all my body weight. I've lost my footing and am hanging from Kris's wrist, my butt on the floor, as I pull him down toward me, desperate to keep him from hurting Beau.

Rudy is frozen, still clutching the hammer, his eyes wide with fear. I try kicking Kris's feet out from under him, but I am too close to get any leverage. I try again, but Kris slashes my arm with the knife. I scream out in pain and let go of his wrist, falling to the floor.

Kris lunges for Beau, pulling the boy up against him. Beau lets out a strangled gasp.

"No! Please! Please!" I beg, getting to my knees, tears streaming down my face. "You can have me. You can have me. Let him go. Please, just let him go. I won't fight you."

Kris watches me, his grip tight on Beau's arm. Tears leak down my face. "Please," I repeat, my voice choked with sobs. "Beau has been such a good boy this year. He deserves presents from... from Santa Claus. Not this. He doesn't deserve this any more than you did."

Kris seems to consider my words. He glances at Beau, and a flicker of something that looks like empathy crosses his painted face.

"Yes," he says softly. "He's been a good boy all year."

He wipes Beau's tears away, leaving streaks of blood on his face. "Come here," he says to me, pointing to the ground in front of him. I hesitate for the briefest of moments, and Kris shouts. "Come here!" I immediately obey, scooting forward on my knees.

Rudy finally snaps out of his frozen state. "Holly, what are you doing?" he asks, his voice trembling.

I speak as I kneel in front of the madman. "Rudy, get Beau out of here."

"Holly, what are you doing?" Rudy repeats, his voice filled with confusion and fear.

"You shut up!" Kris yells, his eyes flashing with rage. Rudy freezes instantly. I take Beau by the shoulders.

"It's going to be okay," I whisper to Beau, trying to sound reassuring. "Go with Mr. Frost. He's gonna get you somewhere safe."

"I don't wanna go," Beau cries, clinging to me.

"I know, baby, but I need you to..." I hug Beau tightly, then push him away gently. "Now go! Go to Mr. Frost. Get Daddy and get somewhere safe. Okay? I love you."

Kris picks up the fallen rope. He wraps the two ends around his hands, a sinister resignation in his eyes.

He tries to loop the rope around my head, but Beau suddenly hugs me again, his small body blocking the rope.

"Mommy, come with me!" Beau cries.

Kris grabs the little boy by the arm and wrenches him away from me, then thrusts him towards Rudy. "Don't make me put you on the naughty list," he says.

"I love you," I call to Beau, my voice breaking.

Beau stumbles as Kris pushes him into Rudy, who suddenly comes unfrozen.

Rudy looks down at Beau, now standing in front of him, and then at me, kneeling in front of Kris, my head bowed, waiting.

He clenches the hammer, his knuckles white as he tightens his grip. Then he yells and swings it at the clown Santa Claus.

Kris reacts immediately, blocking the blow and backing away. The hammer smacks into his arm with a loud thud. I expect to hear a crack. *Shouldn't bones break under such an attack?* But Kris only winces.

"I see you," Kris snarls.

I crawl away from the two men, trying to avoid the swinging hammer and Kris's flailing limbs.

Beau is suddenly snatched from behind by Barry. He has finally made it upstairs, his face pale and strained. He turns Beau towards him. "Downstairs now!" Barry yells.

Rudy swings the hammer again and again, but Kris keeps dodging, a strange, almost playful look on his face. Then, with a swift movement, he catches the hammer in the rope, entangling them both. He pulls, and Rudy stumbles into Kris. Kris grabs him, and Rudy panics, scrambling to get away. Kris laughs, holding onto him, trying to get the rope around his neck, but Rudy is a blur of arms and hands. In his flailing, he knocks the hammer out of Kris's hand. The two men freeze, then leap for the hammer, resuming their wrestling on the floor.

I crawl toward Barry as Kris and Rudy clumsily struggle for control of the hammer. They work their way up off the floor, both of them struggling to get the hammer out of the other's grip. Rudy looks up and throws a punch, but his movements are unpracticed and slow. Kris dodges the blow and then grabs Rudy's arm and pulls hard, making him stumble.

I push myself to my feet. *I've got to help Rudy.* Desperately, I look around for something to use as a weapon, some way to put this psychopath down for good.

Suddenly, Barry starts towards the struggling men. *No!* He's moving very slowly, his breathing labored. I intercept him, putting a hand on his chest. "No!"

"Holly!" Barry gasps, his face pale and drawn.

"Go get Beau and get him out of here!" I plead. "Please. I need the two of you to be safe."

Suddenly, the hammer slams into the back of my head. The impact sends a jolt of pain through my skull, and I see stars.

"Holly!" Barry yells.

I stumble forward, falling to my knees. My head throbs, and a sharp pain shoots through my skull.

Barry looks at Kris, who has thrown the hammer at me. He's now wrestling the rope around Rudy's neck. He finally manages to get it over Rudy's head and pulls it tight, laughing with glee, a high-pitched, chilling sound. "We wish you a merry Christmas and a happy New Year..." he sings, his voice twisted and manic. He stands behind Rudy and pulls on the rope as if he's Santa in his sleigh. "Giddyup!" He hollers at Rudy, giving the rope a shake.

Rudy gags, his hands clawing at the rope.

I try to move, to help him, but I can't get up from my knees. My head is spinning, and my vision is blurry. I sink closer to the floor, trying desperately not to collapse into a useless heap.

Kris starts towards me. Blood trickles down the back of my neck, and I feel numb, unable to react.

Barry moves in front of me, shielding me with his body.

Kris drags Rudy along, keeping the rope taut. Rudy gasps for air, struggling against the rope, his legs fighting to keep him on his feet.

Barry picks up the hammer as Kris reaches him. He swings hard with his one good arm, but his movements are clumsy and slow.

Kris easily catches the hammer and then kicks Barry's feet out from under him. Barry falls to the ground. He jabs the hammer at Kris's knees, but Kris kicks him in the face.

"No!" I whisper, my voice barely audible.

I sag against the wall as Kris digs his hand into Barry's injured shoulder, gouging the gunshot wound. Barry screams in pain.

"Stop it," I whisper again, my voice weak.

"You've all been bad," Kris yells, his voice loud and accusatory. "You're on my list... My naughty list..." he sings, his eyes glinting.

Barry is panting and struggling to rise, using the hammer as a cane rather than a weapon.

Behind Kris, Rudy has managed to loosen the noose and finally gets it over his head. He starts crawling towards the stairs, trying to escape.

Kris suddenly turns, lunges for Rudy, and wraps his arms around him. He grabs the rope and, in one fluid movement, throws it back over Rudy's head.

Rudy struggles to get free, kicking at Kris as he tries to pull the rope off his neck. He begins to cry and beg. "Please. Just let me go. I won't tell anyone. You can have them, just let me go."

Rudy struggles, but Kris holds him tight, wrapping the rope tighter and tighter around him.

Barry helps me to my feet. Rudy is choking and gasping for air.

"From both sides," Barry says to me, indicating that I should go to Kris's right while he goes to the left.

We circle around him, but what should we do? Jump on his back? Grab him around the neck? With the shape we're in, we'd likely wind up being thrown down the stairs.

Kris laughs and suddenly pulls the rope tight. Rudy's face starts to turn purple as he struggles against the rope, choking.

"Rudy!" I scream.

Kris strains to hold the rope tight. Rudy's face turns a dangerous shade of blue.

Barry brings the hammer up and smacks it against Kris's back, but it's as if he doesn't feel it.

"Give it to me," I say, grabbing the hammer from Barry. I swing hard, hitting Kris in his wounded leg. He screams in pain. The rope jerks out of his hands, and Rudy falls to the floor with a thud.

Kris falls to his knees. I swing the hammer again, but Kris catches it and wrenches it out of my hands.

"Barry!" I yell.

But Barry is too slow. *Thwack!* The hammer hits him in the chest, and he crumples to the floor.

I kick Kris in the side, again and again. He curls up, trying to protect himself from my attack, but then he grabs my foot and pulls. I fall forward, landing almost on top of him.

I wrap my arms around him, trying to wrestle him to the ground. I straddle him, trying to pin him down, but I'm too light, too weak.

Kris easily switches our positions, putting himself on top of me and pinning me to the ground. I buck and kick, but he's too strong.

"Just leave us alone! Leave us alone!" I scream.

Kris looks down at me and then covers my mouth with his hand to stop my cries.

He screams at me, his face contorted with rage. "You shouldn't have done it. This is your fault. It's all your fault! You shouldn't have done it."

He releases his hand from my mouth and sinks slowly, lying on my chest as he sobs, his weight crushing me. "You were naughty," he mumbles. "It's your fault."

I lie there, my mouth open, under the sobbing Santa Claus, furious and helpless, aware of the tears leaking out of my own eyes.

I look towards Barry, but he's out cold.

Rudy, still gasping for breath, is crawling towards the stairs, trying to escape.

I look at the knife, even reach for it, but it's entirely out of reach.

I hesitantly pat Kris on the back, mimicking a comforting gesture while cringing inwardly. With a snarl, Kris sits up, his grief replaced with rage.

"And this is what naughty girls get for Christmas," he snarls. He grabs me around the throat and starts to choke me, his fingers digging into my skin. "Silent night, holy night..." he sings, his voice low and sad, like it's a forlorn lullaby.

I grab his wrists, trying to pry his hands from my throat. I gasp for air. "Kris... don't do this," I choke out.

He dissolves into tears again, but doesn't release his hold on me. "You've been bad," he sobs.

I reach up and grab for his eyes, but he pulls his head out of reach, his grip tightening.

"Kris..." I gasp, my face turning purple, my vision blurring.

And then everything goes black.

17
KRIS

Mother's body goes limp under me. Her arms fall to the floor at her sides, and her head turns away from me, resting to one side. This was something new.

Taking my hands from around her neck, I brush my hair out of my eyes and contemplate the woman beneath me. She looks so peaceful, like she's sleeping. I bring my hands up in front of my face and examine them. There are small smudges of blood from Holly's cut on her arm and from my still seeping leg, but the usual coating of blood, the blood dripping down my hands and into my coat sleeves, is missing.

The carpet behind Holly's head is entirely blood-free. I smile, then let out a whoop. I'd done it. There was no mess here. I lay my face down on Holy's chest and breathe deep. No stench of blood in the air. She was dead, but this was definitely different. Better. She'd make the perfect doll. I smile down at Holly, triumphant. *I did it, Mother!*

Then, tears start rolling down my cheeks as despair washes over me. *No! Not again! Mother!* Aching loneliness washes over me at the sight of my dead mother on the floor. *Alone again.*

Mother! The last person who had ever loved me. I sob as I take her in my arms and hold her. I'd never gotten to do this. I'd never gotten to say goodbye. The police had taken me away, and at the funeral, the box had been closed because "no one wanted to see that." But I had. I'd wanted to see her, had desperately wanted to say how sorry I was for pulling away from her, had wanted to tell her how much I missed her and that I loved her.

I hold mom close, sobbing against her such that my tears leave a wet spot on her pajamas. Then I lift her head so I can press my cheek to her cheek. I worry that my stubble will be uncomfortable against her soft skin, but I love how it feels. I keep my cheek against her soft, smaller one and say...

She groans, suddenly, and I yelp and drop her in surprise. She groans again as if the short fall back to the floor hurt her. I laugh at myself. *So, not dead then.*

I hear a noise behind me, and a frown creases my brow. I'd forgotten something. I wipe my face with one sleeve, then get up off the floor, pushing myself up with one hand and using my good leg. My bad leg suddenly hurts a lot. I turn in time to see Mr. Frost disappear down the stairs, the stairs groaning beneath his weight being the sound that has alerted me to his flight.

Holly groans again, and I lift my hands in an exasperated gesture. "Just a minute," I tell her, frowning as she twitches again. This woman is so naughty. *...Like Mom. She looks like Mom, too... and fights like her.* The image of Mom wielding the gun at Dad... Telling him we were leaving... The gun going off... Mom's throat getting cut.

My mood darkens.

First things first. I had to go get old Rudolph to guide my way.

18
HOLLY

A painful throbbing, like a heartbeat, in the back of my head forces me to open my eyes. *What the hell? My head is killing me!* I groan softly at the pain. My throat feels dry and hoarse. I try to clear it, then work to introduce some saliva back into my overly dry mouth. It suddenly dawns on me that I am sitting up, which seems... wrong in light of my throbbing head.

Reluctantly, I open my eyes. They feel like they break open and then can't quite focus. My vision slowly clears, and my surroundings begin to come into focus, along with a memory about... Something...

"Beau?" I whisper, my voice barely audible. I clear my throat and try again, a little louder. "Beau?"

Finally, I can see clearly enough to make out my surroundings. Barry is sitting on the couch across from me, tied up and unconscious. At least, I hope he's unconscious. *Would Kris put him on the couch like that if he were dead?* My chest suddenly feels too tight, and my breathing hitches, coming in short gasps. My vision blurs as I stare at my husband, unsure if he is alive or dead.

A memory surfaces in my groggy mind.

The two of us are driving home through the familiar streets of Havenwood in the soft glow of the dashboard lights. The radio is playing an acoustic version of a song we both used to love, and an easy silence has settled between us, the comfortable quiet of two people who know each other's thoughts without needing words.

Earlier that evening, we'd been at Liam and Chloe's for our Christmas gift exchange. Liam had recounted some ridiculous work story, and Chloe had leaned into him, her hand resting on his arm, her laughter light and genuine. Maya had given Ben an old record, and the two of them were engaged in a familiar, low-key debate about the merits of vinyl versus streaming, their easy bickering a testament to years of comfortable companionship. Even Sarah and Mark, who'd weathered the storms of raising teenagers and demanding careers, still had that unspoken language, a shared glance across the room that spoke volumes of enduring affection. Mark had even reached over and squeezed Sarah's hand as they were leaving, a small, tender gesture that I'd noticed, storing the small gesture away in my memory along with the thought, "I hope that's me one day. Still loved after so many years."

As we left, walking hand in hand to our car, the cool night air crisp against my skin, Barry had squeezed my fingers. "You know," he said, his voice low and warm, a hint of something akin to pride lacing his tone, "out of all of them... I think we're the best couple."

I turned to look at him, a small, genuine smile touching my lips. "Oh yeah?"

He nodded, his gaze earnest in the dim streetlight. "Yeah. We just... fit, you know? We're the most affectionate, the most fun. We don't argue over Christmas gifts..." He paused at the car door, his thumb stroking the back of my hand. "They're all great, our friends, but we... we've got the most going for us. The most love." He said the last word with a slight emphasis, a private joke between us, because I'd been so afraid to admit to myself that I loved him.

He looked at me then, his eyes filled with a genuine tenderness that always made my heart do a little flip. "We're the most in love, Holly. Don't you think so?" There was a vulnerability in his question that had melted me even more.

I'd laughed softly, leaning into him as he opened my door, the scent of his familiar cologne filling my senses. "You're biased."

"Maybe," he'd conceded, a slow, warm grin spreading across his face as he leaned down to brush a stray strand of hair from my cheek. "But I'm right." He'd leaned down and kissed me then, a quick, sweet kiss that lingered just a moment too long, a silent promise of the quiet intimacy that awaited us at home.

A pang of sadness hits me. He'd been wrong. Our friends had all weathered the passage of time and the inevitable wear and tear of life with much greater resilience than Barry and I had. The easy banter, the spontaneous touches, the comfortable silences that used to define us have long since disappeared, overshadowed by the demands of parenthood and the subtle, unspoken resentments and unhappinesses that have grown between us. We've become adept at navigating the logistics of our lives, but the effortless intimacy, the deep connection that Barry had spoken of with such certainty that night, feels like a cherished photograph, just a memory faded by time. But none of that matters now. The petty arguments, the distance, what we used to be... Right now, the only thing that matters is getting him to safety.

Beau!

My brain fog clears a little with the thought of his name. Frantically, I look around the room. *Where is my son?* I find him tied to a small chair in front of the Christmas tree. Kris is crouched in front of him, cooing softly and looking confused about why Beau seems so terrified.

I try to stand, desperate to get to my son, but discover that I am also tied to a chair. I struggle against the ropes, but can't break free. "Let him go!" I yell.

Kris leans towards Beau and caresses his face.

"Don't touch him!" I scream, struggling harder.

"Nice," Kris says, gently.

"Yes. *Nice*. He's nice. Leave him alone!" I yell.

I fight harder against my bonds, but only manage to scoot my chair forward another inch. I sob in frustration. "Beau, honey, I'm right here. Mommy's here."

Kris looks Beau in the eye, and Beau stops crying out of sheer terror.

"I saw Mommy," Kris says, his voice low and creepy. He's explaining something to Beau, but Beau obviously doesn't understand.

I manage to scoot my chair forward another inch, thrashing wildly. I look around the room and then stop, horrified. Rudy is hanging from the balcony. I blanch. The noose around his neck commingles with the long scarf he'd worn to come over, and his face is purple, his eyes bulging.

I look back toward Kris, my mouth hanging open. "What did you do?" I whisper, my voice full of condemnation.

He ignores me.

"Kris. What did you do?" I repeat, my voice strong and demanding. "He was good! On the nice list. You can't hurt people if they're good! Santa Claus gives presents to good boys and girls."

Kris looks at Rudy, and for a moment, he looks sad and ashamed. Then his expression changes, becoming hard and cold once more. "He was naughty," he says.

"You're naughty!" I yell. "That was very bad!"

Something in Kris' expression... a hint of shame... gives me an idea. I continue in my best mom voice. "Now come over here and untie me this instant."

Kris hesitates, then stands and walks over to me. He looms over me, his height exaggerated because I'm stuck in my chair. I lean away from him, uncertain what he will do next, but he just drops to his knees and starts to untie me. *What the hell? I can't believe that worked!* I don't dare to say anything more. Silently, I urge him to continue, but he suddenly puts his head in my lap and starts crying. I just manage to bite my tongue. *No! Come on! Do we have to do this again?*

I steal a glance at Beau, trying to figure out how to get Kris to continue untying me. I decide to continue playing the part of Mom. He's obviously got us confused.

"Sh," I say, trying to comfort him. "It isn't nice to tie up little boys. Would you want to be tied up?"

Kris suddenly jerks his head up off my lap. "I was tied up," He yells. "They locked me in the closet, and they tied my hands. They said I was naughty."

I look at the man on his knees in front of me, and for the first time, I start to see past the makeup. This is a very troubled little boy, his mom murdered in front of him and then abused by... "Who? Who did?" I ask.

Kris lays his head back on my lap. "When you died, they sent me to live with them. They hurt me."

I'm instantly feeling both compassion and rage. Rage at the assholes who hurt a little boy after he'd already been hurt and who helped make him into the kind of man who hurt other people, including my family.

"Kris..." I say, trying to find the right words. But I don't get the chance.

"It was your fault!" He's up and yelling again. "You were bad. Dad told me! He had to put you on the naughty list."

I try one more time. "You could reward the good. You don't have to punish the naughty. You don't have to be like your dad."

Kris leans in close to me, so close I can smell his breath, and says emphatically, "Dad had to do it. You were on the naughty list. Someone has to punish the naughty."

Barry's head suddenly snaps up, and he looks around wildly, his eyes darting from the overturned furniture to the scattered decorations. Then he sees it: Rudy hanging from the balcony, his body swaying slightly, the Christmas lights reflecting off his lifeless eyes.

"Oh my god," Barry whispers, his voice filled with horror.

He looks at Kris, his eyes wide with disbelief and anger. "You killed him? You killed him!"

"HE WAS NAUGHTY!" Kris shouts, making everyone flinch. "Besides, it's her fault," he adds, pointing at me. "Ho! Ho! Ho! Ho! Ho! Ho! Ho! Ho! Ho!" He chants accusingly, using the Santa laugh in chilling mockery.

"*You* killed him!" Barry yells, his voice rising above Kris's chanting. "There's no one to blame but you! And you killed him *here*! In our house. We're gonna have to move!"

Kris suddenly falls silent and grins broadly at Barry. "No, you won't," he says, his voice low and menacing.

"You said Barry and Beau were good!" I say, my voice desperate. "Remember? They're good! They deserve presents, not... to be punished."

"You're good too," Barry says, his eyes filled with worry.

"She's been bad," Kris says, his eyes narrowing.

"Yes. Fine. I've been bad," I say firmly. "But *they've* been good."

"Holly, no!" Barry protests.

"Barry, be quiet," I say, my eyes fixed on Kris. "Let them go. They... They didn't do anything."

Kris starts to laugh, a high-pitched, unsettling sound. "Go? They can't go," he says.

"Why? Why not?" I ask, frustration filling my voice.

"Because..." Kris straightens up importantly. "'Twas the night before Christmas, and all through the house, not a creature was stirring, not even a mouse. The stockings were hung by the chimney with care, and Dad sat right here, while I sat over there," he says, indicating Barry for "Dad" and Beau for himself. Barry stares at the madman, his mouth agape.

"Kris..." I begin, but he cuts me off.

"When out on the lawn, there arose such a clatter, we sprang from our seats to see what was the matter. Out on the driveway, well, who should appear, none other than my sweet, young, mother dear," Kris continues, his voice taking on a sing-song quality.

I glance over my shoulder, looking for the stockings. To my relief, they are close enough to touch. I grab the closest one and pull it up, searching through it, but I don't find what I'm looking for. I shift in my seat, but Kris doesn't seem to notice.

"Her eyes, how they twinkled! Her dimples, so merry! Her cheeks were like roses, her nose like a cherry. But a look in Dad's eye and a twist of his head soon gave me to know I had something to dread," Kris continues, his voice growing darker.

I reach for the next stocking behind me, but I can't quite get it. I shift in my seat again, straining.

"He spoke not a word, but went straight to his work, and Mom struggled and gasped and then died with a jerk. Then, laying his finger aside of her face, he said, 'That's what you get, bitch,' as blood filled the place," Kris finishes, his voice almost gleeful.

The room falls silent. Barry stares at Kris in disbelief. Even I am still, caught up in the ghastly story being told in rhyme.

"The cops sprang from their cars, saw my mom, gave a whistle. Then they took Dad away like the down of a thistle. But I heard him exclaim ere he rode out of sight..."

Kris comes and looks me in the eye. "Your Mom was bad, Kris, and you know that I'm right."

The last sentence is just for me. Kris stays there, looking me in the eye. I force myself not to look away. I know what he wants, but I'm not going to give it to him. Fuck him.

Kris waits, and then finally realizes that I'm not going to admit or confess or whatever it is he's hoping for. His lips lift in a small, amused smile, and he saunters over to Barry. He sits next to my husband, whom just hours ago I would have told you I could live without, and he draws his knife. He puts it up to Barry's neck and looks at me again, a challenge in his eyes.

I shake my head no.

"And so... Now it's Christmas, and I'm here once again..."

He presses the knife into Barry's flesh, and I hear his sharp intake of breath at the pain.

"No!" I beg, unable to think clearly. "No!" He wants something. *What was it?* Tears come to my eyes. Kris seems so resolute.

"...but this time it's to you whom we'll all say amen," Kris says.

"NO! Don't!" I scream. I am vaguely aware of Beau crying. For an agonizing moment, I imagine the blade pulled across Barry's neck, our relationship severed forever. Then Kris lowers the knife.

Air leaves my body in a ragged sigh of relief, and I sag. *That was close.*

Kris walks towards me. I stare up at him uncertainly, and then he wraps his hands around my neck and starts to strangle me.

Barry struggles against his bonds. "No! Stop it!" he yells. "I will break every bone in your body, you psycho!" He stands, but his feet are tied, and he can barely hop towards us. He falls to the floor as I start to turn blue. "Leave her alone!" Barry yells.

Beau starts to scream, his cries piercing the tense silence.

Kris frowns as Beau screams and screams, hardly pausing for breath.

Barry, still on the floor, is untying his feet when Kris suddenly releases me. I gasp for air as he heads for Beau.

"Leave him alone!" I croak.

Kris squats, getting eye level with Beau. Beau's eyes are red and wet, but he stops screaming. He pushes away from Kris, but it only tilts his seat back.

"I'm doing you a favor," Kris says emphatically to Beau. "Do you want me to do it like Dad did? Huh? With all the blood?" Kris starts to cry. "So much blood... Squirting out of her mouth... onto her face and clothes."

He waits for Beau to respond, but of course, he has no idea what the madman is talking about.

Barry has untied his feet. He moves towards me, and I urge him on frantically. "There's a pocketknife in your stocking," I whisper, when he finally reaches me.

Kris is still talking to Beau, his tone soft and mournful, and he looks ashamed. "She crawled towards me... She tried to say something, but the blood sprayed out of her mouth and landed on my arm, and I... I pulled away from her. "

It's as if he's reliving it.

Barry finds the pocket knife in his stocking, but instead of freeing his hands, he starts sawing through the ropes binding my feet.

Kris doesn't seem to remember that we are there. He's completely wrapped up in telling his story. "After that, she lay down on the rug and didn't move anymore, and her blood made a big dark circle in the carpet around her head. She'd have been so mad about that blood on her carpet... Do you want me to make Mom mad and get blood on the carpet?" He asks Beau as if he's expecting an answer.

The ropes at my feet fall away, and Barry starts to work on the ropes at his wrist.

"She looked so pretty under the Christmas tree, though. Like a doll..." Kris says, lost in his memories. "And then Dad started laughing." He switches to a deeper voice, mimicking his father. "Ho, ho, ho! That's what naughty girls get for Christmas. I'm mother fucking Santa Claus."

Kris stays lost in his memories for a moment and then looks at Beau. The little boy is looking at him in horror. Their eyes meet and hold.

Then Kris looks away sadly. "Well, now *I'm* mother fucking Santa Claus," he says quietly.

Barry is sawing vigorously at the ropes around his wrist when Kris suddenly turns and sees him. He looks surprised to find Barry so close to me. "Don't make me put you on my naughty list," he says, pulling out his knife and hurrying towards Barry.

I scream Barry's name, my voice tearing through the air with warning. Barry frantically tries to turn the knife around so he can use it as a weapon against Kris, but his hands are still tied, and he fumbles. The knife falls to the floor, landing with a soft thud on the rug. My stomach drops.

Barry brings his hands up to defend himself as Kris lunges at him with the knife. Still tied to a chair, I lift my legs, which are now free, and kick Kris in the side with every ounce of strength I can muster.

I catch him unaware, and he falls sideways, the knife flying from his hand and skidding across the floor.

The chair I am tied to teeters precariously and then topples to the floor with a crash, landing me painfully on my side.

Barry and Kris both race for the knife, scrambling across the floor, and then wrestling over it in a chaotic mess of limbs and desperation. Each is trying to keep the other from getting to the weapon first.

I tear my eyes away from the men fighting on the floor and focus. I have to get free. Pushing against the bottom stretcher of the chair, I slowly slide the ropes up and over the top of the chair, pushing myself across the floor until all the rope that was binding me to the chair is free. I crawl out of the now loose strands and then look behind me. *Where is it?* I can't see what I'm looking for. My fingers stretch desperately behind me, brushing across the carpet, as I struggle to find the pocket knife behind me. It feels agonizingly close, yet impossibly far.

Barry grabs Kris and tries to push him back, but Kris rolls over and elbows him in the face. Barry's head snaps back, and he grabs his face in pain as Kris crawls over him, reaches out, and grasps the knife. He cries out in triumph, a chilling sound that sends shivers down my spine, then turns, disregarding Barry, and lunges for me.

Barry grabs him around the waist, but Kris just slices his arm with the knife. Barry screams in pain and lets go, clutching his bloody arm.

I search wildly behind me with my hands as Kris starts towards me. My heart pounds in my ears. *Come on! Come on!* Finally, I grasp it, the cold metal comforting in my trembling hand, just as Kris grabs me and pulls me up. Righting my chair, he deposits me into it and presses the knife to my throat. I freeze, every muscle tense, terror gripping me.

"NO!" Barry yells, his voice hoarse with pain and fear.

"Please, Kris," I beg, my voice trembling, tears welling in my eyes.

He starts to cry, the knife shaking against my throat. "Please," I whisper again, my voice barely audible.

"See what you've done?" Kris sobs, his voice laced with pain and accusation.

My eyes dart to the corner of the room. Beau is huddled up in his chair, his small body shaking, his eyes wide with fear as he watches the horrifying scene unfold. *No! I don't want this for him.* My heart aches with guilt and a desperate need to protect him.

"I swear... I'm good..." I choke out, my voice trembling, my gaze flickering to Beau, trying to reassure him, even as I feel the knife blade cut into my skin.

"Why? Why did you have to do it?" Kris cries. "This is all your fault! If you'd just been good... You should have been good." He caresses my face with his free hand, his touch sending shivers of disgust and fear down my spine, but I don't jerk away.

"I was... am good. Kris, look at me," I plead, meeting his gaze. "I have been faithful to..." *Who? Barry? His dad? Who am I in this crazy man's eyes?* "Your dad," I finish lamely.

My eyes flicker back to Beau again. He is still watching, his small face pale and streaked with tears. I try to offer him a reassuring smile, a silent promise that we will get through this. *I have to get free.* I start to cut through the ropes at my wrists, my movements small and careful. I keep my eyes on Kris, who still has the knife at my throat, and try not to let my body sway with the movement of the knife, but I can't keep my arms completely still. I silently pray Kris doesn't notice.

"Please. Just let her go," Barry begs, providing a welcome distraction.

"She's been sleeping with another man! She's been naughty. So naughty!" Kris yells, his voice rising in hysteria.

"I don't know who told you that, but they lied," I say, my voice firm despite my fear. "They lied to you. I would never." I say desperately.

"She's telling the truth." Barry defends me.

"Lying!" Kris screams. "She is lying!"

"Who told you that I was cheating?" I ask, my voice trembling.

Kris leans in close and whispers, singing softly in my ear, "He knows where you are sleeping. He sees why you're awake. He knows that you've been bad, not good."

Silence hangs in the air as we both stare at him in disbelief. Then...

"Kris... You're not Santa Claus. You can't know..." I start to say.

"But I do," Kris says, looking me in the eye in that way again.

Barry suddenly moves towards him, but Kris kicks him in the chest, forcing him backwards. Barry rolls over, fighting to get on his feet, but Kris stops him with his. "Uh, uh, uh." He indicates the knife still at my throat. Barry freezes.

"So be good for your life's sake," Kris finishes, his voice low and menacing.

I lean back in my chair, away from the knife at my throat. I saw viciously through the ropes at my wrists now, desperate to be free, not caring if he notices. "Kris, I haven't cheated," I say. "I've been good. I've been good." I say it over and over again, my voice urgent.

He presses the knife harder against my neck, a burning sensation against my skin. "Liar," he whispers. "Goodbye, mother."

"Please, don't do this," Barry begs, his voice cracking.

Kris looks at Barry, who is lying on the floor, not daring to move. "It's what naughty girls get for Christmas," he says, sadly.

He grabs my hair and pulls my head back sharply, and I let out a small yelp of pain. The sharp edge of the knife presses into my skin, just as I feel the rope break apart behind me. I feel the bite of the blade as I bring my small pocket knife up and stab the small blade into his arm.

Kris shrieks in pain, hopping away from me. He trips over Barry and lands on the couch behind him.

Blood pours down the side of my neck, warm and sticky.

"Holly!" Barry yells as I leap up out of my chair and onto the couch, pocket knife held high. I try to bring it down and stab Kris with it again, but Kris catches my arm, stopping my momentum inches from his body. I've got all my weight above him, pressing the knife towards him, but it isn't enough.

Although our position doesn't change, I can feel him taking control. I scream, holding on with all my might as I feel him ripping the knife from my grasp, and then WHAM! I'm seeing stars. He's elbowed me in the face. I fall off of him with a protest of pain. *How much of this can I take?*

Barry comes at Kris, but Kris punches him in the face. Barry's head snaps back, and he stumbles.

Get up! I order myself, making myself sit up,

Kris grabs a handful of Barry's navy blue hoodie, one of his favorites, although now it has a bullet hole in it and it's covered in blood. Barry tries to get Kris's hands off of him as Kris raises the pocketknife, ready to strike.

"NOOO!" I scream and launch myself off the couch. I crash into Kris' side, but it feels like I've hit a brick wall. He barely stumbles. I reach up, grabbing the hand holding the knife in the air with both of my own, and push against it, successfully stopping Kris from stabbing Barry, but now I've got a tiger by the tail. My arms are stretched above my head, my hands wrapped around Kris's wrist, all my strength going into keeping his hand from descending.

Kris suddenly grabs me around the waist with his free arm and pulls me against him. And then the knife, my knife, the one that was supposed to be my weapon against him, is getting lower and lower, closer to me. *No!* I push with all my strength, straining, my two hands to his one, to keep the knife away from me, but to no avail. Steadily, it descends, getting closer and closer, until the knife touches my stomach with a sharp poke and then pushes inside me.

I watch in disbelief as the blade punctures my skin, even as I scream at the hot, blinding pain that burns from where I've just been stabbed. Kris backs away from me, looking shocked and ashamed.

"See what you made me do?" He screams, looking like he's about to cry. He starts to moan and fret as I fall onto the couch, holding the handle of the knife protruding from my stomach. *Do I pull it out? No, right? I'm supposed to leave it in.*

Kris comes towards me, his tall figure looming over me as I lie on the couch. He keeps mumbling to himself. "Naughty. Naughty!" I get the impression that he wants to comfort me, but I fucking don't care. With a cry of pain, I kick him hard in his bad leg, the one with the bullet hole in it. Kris drops to the ground, screaming in pain.

Barry hurries over and digs his foot into Kris's bad leg, and he moans even louder, writhing in pain under Barry's foot, but Barry doesn't let up. "Get the knife." He orders me, and I look around, but I don't see it.

"Here." I start to pull the small knife out of my stomach, but Barry stops me.

"No, not that one. You could bleed out," he says, looking around.

I turn to look for Kris' knife when suddenly Kris kicks Barry's leg out from underneath him. Barry goes down, and I run to intercede, but Kris reaches up, grabs the knife protruding from my stomach, and yanks it out of me. I give an ungodly yelp at the pain, but Kris doesn't hesitate; he climbs on top of Barry and plunges the knife into Barry's shoulder.

Barry screams.

"No!" I yell for like the 5th time that night. Now that he's weaponless, I leap at Kris, pushing hard against his chest. He falls backwards off of Barry and onto the floor. I end up on top of him, he on his back, and the two of us stomach to stomach. His legs are bent, trapped underneath his own body, and he struggles to free them as I climb over him, get to my feet, and head for the stairs.

Gotta get him away. Away. Away from Barry and Beau. They keep getting hurt, and it's my fault.

I glance behind me to make sure Kris is following and yelp as I find him right on my heels, both of us limping in pain as we round the corner around the staircase and start up the stairs. I use the handrail to help propel me forward. I can't move fast enough, can't make my body move any faster. I can hear Kris struggling up the stairs behind me, so close, I swear I can feel him breathing down my neck.

I make it to the top of the stairs, winded and about to pass out from pain. I've never been stabbed before. The pain is intense. I wonder briefly how Kris is managing so well with a bullet wound. But then, he probably doesn't feel normal things like pain.

I force myself to move faster as my end goal comes into sight. *Just a little further!* I can feel Kris right behind me, can almost feel his hands wrapping around me. I run for all I'm worth to the safety of the closest door. It's the bathroom. I leap through the doorway and turn. I catch a glimpse of Kris, his face determined as he lunges for me... but he's too slow.

19
HOLLY

I slam the bathroom door shut and twist the lock. The door shudders under the force of a heavy thump as Kris flings himself against the other side. I flinch, stumbling back, my eyes glued to the door as if it might splinter apart at any second. He pounds on the door, rattles the handle, then starts to kick. He kicks the door again and again. It groans and shudders under the force of his blows, but it holds.

My chest heaves, each breath sharp and shallow, as if the air itself is too thick to swallow. I turn to the mirror, and my breath catches in my throat. Blood. So much blood. It streaks down my neck in dark, glistening rivulets, staining the collar of my pajamas. My hands are slick with it, and it's soaking into my pajama top where he's stabbed me in the side.

Trembling, I grip the edge of the sink. My reflection stares back at me—pale, wide-eyed, and wild. I look like a ghost, or maybe a corpse. The kind of thing you'd see in a horror movie. The thought makes me want to laugh, but a hysterical sob escapes me instead. Pulling myself together, I tear open the cupboard, my fingers fumbling over bandages, gauze, and bottles of antiseptic.

The kicking at the door continues, each thud sending a jolt of terror through me but also reassuring me that he's still here. Barry and Beau are safe... for the moment, at least. I silently pray that Barry gets Beau out of the house, but then doubt he'll leave me to do it.

I press a gauze pad to the wound on my neck, sucking in air at the pain, then wrap a bandage around my neck, tight enough to make my head throb, but I don't care. I have to stop the bleeding. I have to keep moving.

Lifting my pajama top, I wince at the sight of the gash in my side. The edges are ragged, the skin around it already bruising. My stomach churns, but I force myself to press another pad to it, wrapping the bandage around my waist.

The kicking suddenly stops, and the sudden silence is worse than the noise. My heart pounds in my ears as I stare at the door, waiting, listening. *Is he still out there?* I press my ear against the wood. Nothing. No sound. No movement. Just... silence.

I hesitate. *Maybe it's a trap. He could be standing out there just waiting for me to open the door.* I listen again, but hear nothing. *Did he leave?* My heart suddenly races. *Is he going after Barry and Beau? I* can't just open the door. What if he's standing there? *A weapon. I need something...* But I'm in a bathroom.

I start searching through the lotions and hair brushes. *What? What can I use?* I start to despair at the half-empty bottles of shampoo and soaps, and then I see it, a bottle of aerosol hairspray. I grab it and pop off the lid. It's something.

I walk to the door, my hand hovering over the lock. I hesitate, listening, then twist it and yank the door open, spraying the hairspray into the air in front of me. The hallway is empty. The eerie silence of the house is broken only by the sound of my own ragged breathing.

Holding my side, I tiptoe forward, peering around the corner and down the dark hallway between the upstairs bedrooms. I search the shadows, but they are empty. I creep to the balcony, peering down over the railing into the living room. Also empty. Barry and Beau are gone, and there is no sign of Kris. My mind races, panic clawing at the edges of my thoughts, but I force myself to move slowly. I have to find Barry and Beau.

I start down the stairs, moving faster as I get to the bottom. *Just have to make it to the bedroom.* By the time I get there, I'm running, my mind imagining all kinds of horrors just behind me. I tear the bedroom door open, race inside, shut the door, and twist the lock. I'm suddenly aware of someone behind me. I turn, ready to defend myself. Barry nearly takes my head off with Kris' knife. I throw up my hands, whispering furiously, "It's me! It's me!"

He lowers the knife, his face pale and drawn. "You scared the shit out of me."

"Where is he?" I ask, my voice barely above a whisper.

"He went into the garage. I was just coming up to get you."

We both freeze as the garage door creaks open, then closes. Footsteps echo on the stairs, slow and deliberate. My stomach twists. *I left the bathroom door open.* He'll know I'm not there in a matter of seconds. I step further into the bedroom, searching frantically, then run to our dresser.

"Come on," I say to Barry, positioning myself at one side of the dresser. Barry hurries to the other side, and we lift, both of us gasping with the effort of lifting the solid wood dresser with our injuries. We unceremoniously deposit it in front of the bedroom door, both of us breathing hard, trying to recover. *We can't take much more of this.*

I turn and see Beau hiding behind the bed, and my heart breaks. My poor baby. *How will he ever feel safe again?*

Suddenly, we hear footsteps on the stairs. They echo through the house, coming down, down, down. The footsteps get louder and closer. Kris is heading right for us. He's heard us. He knows where we are.

I run to Beau, wrapping my arms around him. "I'm so sorry, honey. Are you okay?"

Before he can answer me, an axe hits the door with a deafening thud, its shiny tip just showing through the wood of our bedroom door. Beau screams, and I jump to my feet, looking around the room for something, anything, to use as a weapon. But there is nothing. Just the sound of the axe tearing through the wood, little splinters flying into the room.

Barry is standing between us and the door, the knife in his hand, blood soaking his shirt where his gunshot wound is still seeping.

"Why don't we have a gun?" I yell over the noise of the axe hitting the door.

"Well, obviously, we're getting one now," he replies, his voice tight with pain.

The axe comes through again, and Beau screams louder.

I stand, facing the door, watching the hole in the door get bigger and bigger, when, suddenly, it hits me. "It's me he wants," I whisper the realization out loud.

I rush into our closet and grab my winter coat and boots.

"What are you doing?" Barry asks, concerned, but I don't answer.

I head to the nightstand, where I suddenly know my cell phone is charging, and grab my phone. *Of course, the one time it's where it's supposed to be.* I shove it into my pocket and hurry to the end of the bed, where I sit and pull on my boots and coat.

I can see Kris through the small hole he has already chopped into our bedroom door. The axe continues to strike again and again. Our bedroom floor is a mess of wood chips and paint. Kris peers in, his face splitting into a grin. "Ho, ho, ho! It's Santa Claus!"

Barry asks me again, "What are you doing?"

"It's me he wants," I say softly so Kris can't hear us through the hole in our door. The sound of the axe helps cover our conversation. "I'm going to lead him away. Once I'm gone, go get help." My voice is steady despite the fear clawing at my chest. "You should be able to track me from your laptop."

"Holly, this is crazy!" Barry says, desperately.

"It isn't crazy. This will work, and you know it." I suddenly feel calm for the first time tonight. I finally have a plan. I'm taking charge.

"Don't do this!" Barry pleads.

"It's the only way."

"You're hurt."

I laugh, a bitter, hollow sound. "Yeah. But so is he."

Kris is pulling chunks of the door away now, his face twisted with manic glee. He can already get his head and shoulders through the hole in the door.

I rush over to Beau, crouching down so I'm at his eye level. I grab his face, looking fiercely into his eyes. "I love you with my whole heart, and I am so proud to be your mother. I'm so sorry for this. Don't let it ruin anything. Live a beautiful life."

I turn to Barry, "I'm so sorry for everything."

"Don't do this," he whispers.

We're pulling into our driveway, the familiar crunch of tires on gravel a comforting sound. The porch light casts a warm glow on our little house, a beacon of safety after a pleasant evening with friends. We walk hand in hand up the path, the easy rhythm of our steps in sync.

Just as I reach for the doorknob, Barry turns me to face him, his hand still holding mine, his eyes suddenly filled with a playful intensity. Before I can even register his intent, he's kissing me, a sudden, fervent kiss that steals my breath away. It's not a polite peck; it's a deep, hungry kiss that speaks of desire.

He presses me back against the wooden support post of our porch, the rough texture digging slightly into my back. His hands move from mine to cup my face, his thumbs tracing the curve of my cheekbones. The kiss deepens, his tongue tangling with mine, a familiar dance that sends a shiver of longing through me.

Then his hand slips lower, tracing the line of my hip, and then, with a boldness that makes my heart pound, it slides up under the hem of my skirt, his fingers caressing my bottom. A gasp escapes my lips, a mixture of surprise and a familiar thrill. A nervous laugh bubbles up. "Barry! The neighbors!" I whisper, glancing self-consciously at the darkened houses on either side.

He just chuckles, a low rumble against my lips, his eyes dark and intent. "Don't care." His grip tightens slightly, a possessive gesture that ignites a familiar spark within me. The thrill of the forbidden.

The raw desire in his eyes is intoxicating, and the world outside our little bubble fades away. The cool night air, the quiet suburban street, none of it matters. There's just Barry, his hands on me, his lips on mine. Finally, breathless and flushed, we break apart, a shared smile lingering between us. An unspoken promise hangs in the air, thick with anticipation. We walk inside, still hand in hand, the energy between us palpable.

We haven't been like that in what feels like a lifetime. I'm not sure how we would even find our way back to that. A profound sadness washes over me at the time we've wasted keeping score and waiting for the other person to make a move. *And now it might be too late.*

"I love you," I say for the first time in... I can't remember how long.

"I love you too." And I suddenly know he means it.

I turn to leave, but Barry stops me. "Here," He says, placing the knife into my hand. "Take this."

"Good idea."

I run to our bedroom window and throw it open. The freezing night air hits me in the face, and a few small snowflakes flutter inside. Half of Kris's body is through the door now. He's trying to pull himself through the too-small opening. I turn, looking back at the insane scene unfolding in my bedroom, and smile. Kris's eyes lock with mine, a 'don't you dare' expression in their depths, but my smile only widens. "See ya, psycho," I say, and then I climb out the window.

20
KRIS

The axe hits the door with a satisfying thunk. The tip sinks into the wood and goes, I believe, all the way through to the other side. I rip the axe out of the door, swing it behind me, and back around. Thunk! It hits with the sound of wood splintering.

It feels so good. The heavy axe in my hands, the swinging motion in my arms. This might become my new weapon of choice. So much more satisfying than a blade across a throat. Such a small motion, with such small results. A little gurgle, some spewed blood... I hit the door again. Yes. Definitely going to have to try this on my next victim.

A sad, forlorn feeling comes over me at the thought of having to wait an entire year. I sigh. But that is how Christmas works, and I am Santa Claus. It's my job to prepare all year before going out into the world and spreading my Christmas cheer.

Light shines through the several small holes I have punctured in the door. I can hear the little boy screaming. It hurts me... his pain, his terror, feels so familiar, so raw. I focus my efforts on one spot on the door and watch, satisfied, as the small opening grows larger and larger. I can hear mom and dad arguing, then whispering as the hole gets bigger. They're being naughty!

I swing the axe harder, and suddenly the hole is as big as my face. Big enough to see inside. I put my face into the hole and peer in. Mom is putting on her coat and boots. My brow furrows. *What does she need those for?*

Dad is holding my knife. *Naughty! That's my knife!* The need to take it away from him, to reclaim it, comes over me like a rash, an itch that can only be scratched or sated when I am whole again, the knife and I reconnected. But while I want my knife, I am still enjoying the feel of the axe in my hand, its significant weight, the large swinging motion... I know I won't be able to let it go. It's going to be part of me now. A new addition. *Maybe I'll use the axe to get in just for fun and then use the knife.*

I poke my head through the opening in the door. "Ho! Ho! Ho! It's Santa Claus!" I announce. The little boy screams, and Mom and Dad glance at me, then continue arguing. My brow furrows deeper. I feel dismissed, and I don't like it.

The little boy starts crying, and Mom rushes over to him. She takes his face in her hands, and she says something to him. I strain to hear what it is. It feels very important. *What is she saying?*

I scream in frustration and take another swing at the door. *Have to get inside.* I look at the little boy as Mom stands and moves away from him. His face is sad, but he's gotten something I didn't: a final moment with Mom.

If I just hadn't pulled away... If Dad hadn't slit your throat and you could have told me... What would you have said?

I scream in frustration and try to pull myself through the opening in the door. I've made it slightly larger, but not quite big enough to fit through. I push at the weakened chunks around the hole, trying to get myself through, but my Santa suit keeps getting caught on the jagged edges of the opening. I scream again.

I hear Mom tell Dad that she loves him. *Wait. That's not right. Do you love someone you're cheating on?* Then Dad says he loves her, too, and I whimper. *Do you love someone and then slit their throat?*

Dad raises the knife, and for a moment, I'm afraid the past is going to repeat itself, and he is going to do just that, slit her throat for lying, but he just hands it to Mom. *Doesn't he know she's naughty?* Mom takes the knife and walks across the room.

What is she doing? She pushes open a window, grips the windowsill, and puts one foot up on a nightstand. *She's leaving? She can't leave! I'm doing all of this for her... To make it better... for her. I won't leave any blood on the carpet this time!* I think as I struggle harder to get to her. *Please! Don't go! I have to finish this!*

But I can only scream with the effort of trying to push myself through the door, desperate to reach her in time. She hesitates, then turns back and looks me in the eyes. She smiles at me and says, "See ya, psycho!" And then she climbs out the window.

21

HOLLY

Our bedroom is on the second floor. I refuse to look down as I put the knife between my teeth, then carefully climb out the window, onto the small windowsill. The night air is bitterly cold, and the wind bites at my skin.

Kris struggles to pull himself through the jagged hole he's carved in our bedroom door. "No!" He screams. "No!" His breath comes in ragged gasps, his eyes wild and unfocused, and I silently pray that this works, that he runs past Barry and Beau and follows me out into the night. If we're lucky, he'll fall and break both his legs, and this will all be over. If we're unlucky, I'll fall and break both of my legs.

Kris struggles a moment longer, straining to get in, then suddenly changes direction. Instead of trying to get into the room to come after me, he starts pushing himself back out the small opening. He's figured out where I'm going and plans to meet me there.

Barry sees it too and grabs Kris by the arm. "Not so fast, you son of a bitch," Barry growls, his voice strained but fierce. The two men start to wrestle, Kris trying to get away while Barry holds him fast.

My hands tremble as I grip the window frame, my knuckles white with the strain. The knife is still clutched in my teeth. Slowly, I stretch one leg towards our front porch. It's built up to be level with the second story of the house and is my intended escape route. I don't look down; instead, I focus on the porch ledge, which is a good 3 feet away. My foot reaches the porch wall, and I tentatively shift my weight. My foot suddenly slips, and I can't help but let out a small shriek of fear and surprise. The knife falls out of my mouth and disappears into a snowbank below. *Shit!* My fingers manage to keep their grip on the window frame, and I force myself to calm down and start again.

I catch a glimpse of Barry just as Kris punches him in the face. Barry stumbles back, releasing Kris and moaning in pain.

Finally free, Kris rears back, his face contorting with rage. He raises the axe, the blade glinting in the dim light, and brings it down in a vicious arc. The axe sinks into the dresser with a deafening thunk, wood splintering everywhere, but he is still trapped in the door, so the swing lacks momentum.

Barry gets his footing and puts one hand on his face where Kris just hit him. His chest is heaving, but he is still trying to buy me time. "That's right, asshole. Come and get me," he taunts, his voice shaking but defiant.

Kris doesn't take the bait, only renews his efforts to back himself out of the hole in our bedroom door.

I have to get out of here! Slowly, carefully, I inch my way closer to the far side of the window. My breath is coming in shallow gasps. The ground below seems very far away. I stretch out one leg and, again, get my boot on the ledge. I push it a little farther, hoping to make it secure this time. Slowly, I transfer my weight from the foot on the windowsill to the foot on the ledge, one knee bending as the other knee straightens. I reach for the wall, grasping onto it with my right hand and then pulling myself up. My hand holds, and I bring my other hand to the porch wall, lifting myself up and over. I've made it. My feet land on the wooden planks of the porch with a soft thud. My heart is racing, but I feel triumphant.

I hear him before I see him. His footsteps pound on the hardwood floor as he barrels towards the front door. He slams into the small rectangular window next to it, and I jump, my heart leaping into my throat. Kris stands there, his face twisted with rage, his eyes locked onto mine through the window. The Christmas lights cast a sickly glow around him, making him look like some kind of deranged holiday demon.

I stumble backwards, my hands grasping for the railing but never quite finding it. Then he rips the door open, and I turn and flee, clinging to the railing as I hurry down the icy stairs towards the driveway.

My side is on fire as I reach the bottom step, but Kris isn't moving any faster than I am with a bullet wound in his leg. The two of us limp along in the world's slowest chase. "Here comes Sant-a. Here comes Sant-a," Kris sings behind me and then laughs at his own humor.

I make it to the bottom of the stairs and start towards the driveway, mindful of the ice beneath my feet. Big fat snowflakes lazily make their way through the night sky. The streetlights glow in the distance, a beacon of safety, and I head towards them. I just need to get to someone's house, and I'll be safe. *Or they'll be dead.* I recoil at the thought still running. I make it to my driveway and have to slow down. It's completely covered in ice. I can't risk a fall.

Okay, who is my biggest, most intimidating neighbor? But something whistles through the air. I hear it coming toward me and duck instinctively. The axe embeds itself in the ground just inches from where I'd been standing. I veer away from the hurtling missile and up the driveway instead of down, heading toward the back of the house, away from the lights, away from safety.

The yard is a blur of shadows as I run, my ragged breaths white in the air. The snow in the yard is deep, and my legs burn as I run and leap, trying to make my way through it. Icy snow falls into the top of my boots and melts down my legs and onto my feet, but there's no helping it. I reach the hill behind the house and scramble up, my boots slipping up the incline. At the top, I stop, turning to look back at the quiet neighborhood just out of reach. *So close!*

Kris comes around the side of the house. The axe in his hand. He stops when he sees me, leaning against the house as he catches his breath. His face is pale, his eyes wild.

Something inside me knows I've taken control, taken over the game, and I feel exultant. "On the twelfth day of Christmas, my victim escaped me!" I sing, my voice shaking but defiant. I laugh, the sound manic and unhinged, even to my own ears. "You're too late! You missed me! It's no longer Christmas Eve. Your sweet mother was already dead by now. You've screwed it all up!"

He stares at me, his expression darkening. I smile at him, triumphant, but instead of coming after me, he turns and heads for the back door of the house. *What's he doing? He is not going back inside!*

"I don't know what you're blaming your mother for anyway," I shout, my voice carrying through the cold night air. "This whole thing is your dad's fault. What kind of psycho kills his wife for cheating? He could have just divorced her or forgiven her. Did you ever think of that? It's his fault you were in the system. His fault you didn't have a mother. His fault he got taken to prison. In fact, it's his fault your mom cheated in the first place because he was obviously a terrible person! So, all of this!" I indicate him, myself, my house, everything. "His fault!"

Kris pauses at the back door, his hand on the knob. I can see the tension in his shoulders, the way his grip tightens. *I'm winning.* I don't hold back, even though I realize that it could have all gone differently for him. He could have had a normal life, with ups and downs just like the rest of us. "You're just lucky that your mother died before she could see what a terrible son she has..."

That does it. He turns, his face contorted with rage, and leaps toward me, running as fast as his injured leg will carry him. *Shit.* I stumble back, my heart pounding as I scramble up the rest of the hill. The fields stretch out behind the house, dark and endless, but I don't stop.

In my pajamas, coat, and boots, I run. The sound of him struggling through the snow behind me drives me forward, faster and faster, until I disappear into the shadows of the fields. The snow crunches under my boots, and the wind whips at my face, but I don't dare look back. I can hear him, his breathing ragged, his footsteps uneven, but he is still coming. Still chasing me.

I veer left, toward the tree line, hoping to lose him in the woods. The trees loom ahead, their branches skeletal against the night sky. I plunge into the darkness, the snow deeper here, slowing me down. My legs burn, and my side aches where I've been stabbed, but I push through the pain. I have to keep going. I have to get away.

Behind me, I hear him stop, his footsteps faltering. I risk a glance over my shoulder and see him standing at the edge of the trees, his chest heaving, the axe hanging loosely at his side. He stares into the woods, his face unreadable in the darkness. For a moment, I think he might give up. But then he raises the axe and steps forward, his eyes locking onto mine.

"Dashing through the snow," he sings, "On a one good, working leg. Over the fields we go. Laughing all the way. Ho! Ho! Ho!" His voice echoes through the trees. "What fun it is to laugh and sing a slaying song tonight."

I turn and run deeper into the woods, my heart pounding in my chest. The trees close in around me, their branches clawing at my coat, but I don't stop. At least he's no longer at my house with Beau.

22

KRIS

I come around the side of the house, the axe heavy in my hand, its weight comforting. I'd had to dig it out of a snow bank after throwing it.

My leg screams with every step, the bullet wound throbbing like a second heartbeat. It feels... interesting. I lean against the house, my chest heaving, my breath coming in ragged gasps that fog the cold night air. My eyes lock onto Holly, standing at the top of the hill, her silhouette framed by the pale moonlight. She looks small from here, fragile, but I know better. She's strong. Very strong.

She starts singing and laughing, and even to my ears, she sounds crazy and manic. My chest tightens, and for a moment, I can't breathe. *What's wrong with Mom?* She's out here in the middle of the night, and it's freezing! A small voice inside me answers... *She's leaving! She's leaving you alone... again.*

I don't want her to go. The urge to chase her down, catch her, and force her to come help me make things right is surging through me, but I'm cold, and my leg hurts. An idea formulates in the back of my brain, and a small smile curves my lips upwards. *She won't leave them... if I go back in, she'll come.* I turn away from her, my eyes darting to the back door of the house. *Dad and I are inside. Mom would never leave me.* I walk to the back door and reach for the handle. I can almost feel Mother panic behind me, and then her voice rings through the cold night air.

I freeze, my hand on the doorknob. She's yelling, her voice carrying through the crisp night air, saying mean things about Dad. *No, no, no! Stop! Dad will hear you!* My breath hitches, my chest tightening like a vice as her words echo in my head, twisting and turning, digging into places I don't want them to go. Dad's face flashes in my mind—cold and angry, and I hear his voice, sharp and cruel. *Your mom's bad, Kris!*

I shake my head to silence him, but Mom... no, Holly is still yelling. "And you're just lucky that your mother died before she could see what a terrible son she has..."

Something inside me snaps, a raw, primal rage surging through me like a wildfire. I turn, my face contorted with fury, my eyes locking onto Holly. She's standing up there on the hill, wreathed in shadow. Her hair is wild and blowing in the wind. She looks like a crazed demon. Mom would never let her hair get so mussed. No. This was definitely Holly. And she's been bad. *Naughty girl,* I think, my grip tightening on the axe. *Naughty, naughty girl.*

I leap towards her, my injured leg screaming in protest, but I don't care. The pain doesn't matter. Nothing matters except making her stop. She has to stop saying mean things about mom... and dad. She stumbles back, her eyes widening as she scrambles up the hill, but I'm going to catch her. We both know it's inevitable. I'm Santa Claus, and it's my night.

The fields are an endless expanse of snow. I run and run, but Mother keeps getting farther away from me. *Wait, Mother! Come back!* I whimper. *Don't leave me!* I feel like a little boy again, sitting under the Christmas tree and watching the life seep out of her onto the carpet, helpless and afraid. *Come back!* I growl. *I need you!*

I can hear her up ahead, her boots crunching in the snow, her breath coming in ragged gasps. She's slowing down. I'm propelled forward, clear that I would chase her to the ends of the earth. *I have to make it right. No Blood.* The axe feels light in my hand now, like an extension of my arm.

Mother veers left, toward some trees, and I follow, my chest heaving, my leg still pounding with the rhythm of my heartbeat. The trees cast dark shadows, their sharp, empty branches still creating cover in the dark. She plunges into their midst, disappearing into the shadows ahead of me, but I'm not worried. I can hear her, the snow crunching under her boots and her loud gasping breaths.

At the edge of the woods, I pause to catch my breath, my chest heaving, the axe hanging loosely at my side. I stare into the trees, my eyes scanning the darkness. For a moment, I think I've lost her, but then I catch a flash of movement between the trees. My lips curl into a smile.

"You can't run forever, Mother," I say, and then hurry after her.

23
HOLLY

My side burns, and I stop for a moment, bending over to catch my breath. I place a hand over my stab wound, trying to apply pressure. I can feel it bleeding through the bandage underneath my coat and pajamas. Behind me, I can hear him, my Kris Kringle killer. His footsteps are heavy, uneven, but relentless. He's gaining on me. *How is that possible? I shot him in the leg!* But it's true. I whither at the unwelcome reminder of men's dominant strength. *I'll just have to play smarter.*

I look around for a way out, a weapon, anything that might give me an advantage. The moon hangs high above, casting an eerie glow over the snow-covered field. I'm struck by the beauty of it. It's the kind of beauty that makes you forget, for a moment, that you're running for your life. The sound of Kris's labored breathing and the occasional thud of the axe dragging through the snow bring the fact sharply back into focus.

I need to get out of these woods and back to civilization. Someplace to get help. I've been running in the direction of what I hoped was our neighborhood, but I'm either not covering enough ground, or I've gotten turned around in the woods. It's impossible to move in a straight line through the trees, bushes, and branches. Instead, I've been choosing the easiest path through them in the hopes of moving faster.

I glance over my shoulder, my heart pounding in my chest. Kris is behind me, his figure a dark shadow moving through the trees, his movements jerky but determined. The axe glints in the moonlight, and for a moment, our eyes meet. He looks at me almost sadly, as if somehow it's me hurting him, and then his expression changes, and I realize, he's not going to stop. He's never going to stop.

24
KRIS

My leg has been burning for a while now. I can feel the blood running down my leg and into my boot. *Why is she running? Doesn't she know I'm doing this for her?* I ignore both the pain and the blood. If I can't run, I'll skip. I do a little hop, but it's hard in the snow. I giggle at my own awkwardness and try again. *Yes! Skip, step, skip, step.*

The trees with their bare branches are doing little to hide her, but it's dark, and I can't miss my chance. "It's no longer Christmas Eve." I hear her voice echoing in my head. She's being bad, messing everything up. She's supposed to be under the Christmas tree by now. All dressed in her pretty dress, with her makeup on. Maybe she doesn't know about the makeup, or maybe she's still worried about the blood. I suddenly realize I forgot to tell her that there won't be any blood this time. I hit my head with an open hand. *Stupid. Stupid! Of course! She's worried about the blood getting on the carpet!*

My other hand feels heavy, and I look to see why. I'm holding an axe. I remember picking it up and then using it to chop through the door. *So thrilling!* I've never used an axe. *It's not what Dad used,* I think to myself, and my shoulders slump. I should probably throw it away. Dad might be mad I'm using it. But then, Dad had used glass. Maybe the important thing was cutting the throat. I like this reasoning because it means I get to keep my new axe. I give it a good swing. It feels so good, so right, I just want to sink it into her... *Wait! I can't kill her with this. There would be blood! So much blood. More blood, even.*

I giggle. *More blood!* Mom would be even more mad. But then, suddenly, I realize if I kill her outside, there won't be any blood on the carpet! I don't think Mom would care about blood in the snow.

I have to catch her. If the sun comes up, it will be too late. Suddenly, I hear a small scream. I search the darkness ahead, but don't see her. I keep moving in the direction of that small unconscious shriek and then... I see her flailing on the ground. She's fallen.

I move faster. This is my chance. She tries to stand up, but her foot is caught. She pulls at her boot, tugging desperately, but it stays stuck.

I race up to her and then stop, looming over her. Her face becomes a familiar mask of fear and desperation. It's so beautiful. I decide to straddle her to keep her still. My knees land in the snow on either side of her, but the feel of her beneath me is surprising. I... like it. I hesitate, enjoying the feeling.

She grabs a nearby stick and swings it, hitting me in the face. The blow breaks the stick into pieces. It's enough to turn my head. She takes advantage of her opening, bucking wildly, then pushing me off of her. I enjoy the feeling of her squirming beneath me, even as she escapes.

Naughty! Dad's voice reprimands me for my pleasure, and I whimper. *But it's not Mother. It's Holly,* I tell the voice, arguing with Dad even as Holly gets to her feet. *I can't let her escape.* I dive for her foot, barely grabbing it as she starts to run. She falls again, snow flying from the impact. I crawl up her body as she kicks and pushes at me. I remember not to like it this time. Although I can't seem to help it.

She bucks and struggles, and enjoying it so much is making me feel... dirty. I glare at the woman beneath me. *It's her fault.* "Ho, ho, ho," I whisper. She is so naughty.

She's too close for me to swing my axe the way I want to, so I wrap my hands around her neck. She picks up a small stick, and I laugh. *What's she going to do with that? It's too small to...* She jabs it into my eye, and my eye explodes in pain. I scream, grabbing my face and rearing back. The stick is still protruding from my face. I try to gently pull it out, but Holly won't stop moving. I lift myself off of her, letting her escape, then slowly, gently, pull it out. It comes easily, but with a *schlupping* sound that gives me goosebumps. Not too deep then. But I can't see. Can't open either of my eyes.

How could she do this to me? The pain is... intense.

I pull my hand away from my face and look at it through one watery eye. It's covered in blood. "Naughty," I say out loud, but Holly's already on her feet, already running away from me. *I mustn't lose her. What would Dad say?*

I struggle to my feet, pain shooting down my wounded leg. My injured eye is unopenable. With my one good eye, I look through the darkness for movement. *There! I see her.* I leap forward despite the pain, after all, pain is something I am very familiar with.

25
HOLLY

The woods are a blur of shadows and snow. I don't dare look back. My heart is racing. *I just stuck a stick in a man's eye.* He'll probably never be able to use it again. Guilt and pain fill me. I'm surprised by my reaction. This psycho is trying to kill me, and I feel bad about putting a stick in his eye? What if it came down to him or me? What if I have to kill him to save my own life?

I strengthen my resolve. I'll do it if I have to. I'll kill him, but I somehow know that doing so will haunt me for the rest of my life.

I look behind me, but I can't see him. Relief floods through me. Maybe a stick in the eye was just what I needed. I look around for a hiding place. If I hide, he might pass by me. I could circle back around and go home. By now, Barry will have the police there, right? *How long has it been?* It feels like I've been out here running for hours.

I look for a tree big enough to hide behind, but there aren't a lot of good options, nothing big enough that I won't poke out on one side. I start to panic as the seconds tick by. Kris has steadily gained on me all night. I don't have much time. I don't know how fast he can move with only one eye, but a bad leg has barely slowed him down. I pick a tree and duck behind it, my chest heaving. I press myself against the trunk, listening for sounds of pursuit.

At first, the only thing I hear is the pounding of my own heart, but then I hear snow crunching underfoot and the faint rustle of branches. *He's close. Too close.* I calm my breathing, taking short, shallow breaths. I can't have him hear or see it. I cover my mouth with my hands, trying to discourage the white clouds escaping my lips.

I peek around my tree, and Kris comes into view, his movements slow and deliberate. He stops several yards away, his head tilted as if listening.

I don't dare move as he turns in a slow circle, his one good eye scanning the trees. For a moment, I think he might walk right past me, but then he hesitates, listening again. My heart skips a beat, and I hold my breath, waiting.

And then, suddenly, my cell phone rings.

The sound is deafening in the silence, and I fumble with my pocket, my fingers numb and clumsy. I pull the phone out, my hands shaking, and try to silence it, but instead, I accidentally answer.

"Hey, baby. You alone? Can you talk?" a male voice says, smooth and familiar.

No, no, no!

I stab at the screen, eyes wide in terror as I try to hang up. I can feel Kris watching me. *What is he waiting for?* I look up from my phone, scrambling to put it back in my pocket. I have to have it. It's the only way they can find me.

Kris is still standing there. He smiles, a cold, cruel smile, then raises the axe and runs right at me. I scream and duck, sliding down the tree trunk as the axe slams into the wood above me, exactly where my head had been just seconds ago. The impact sends a shower of splinters raining down over me. I cover my head, then look up. Kris is trying to pull the axe free of the tree. I gather my wits and kick him in his wounded thigh. I almost kick his leg out from under him. Kris screams, then, almost without looking, backhands me across the face.

The world spins. I land face down in the snow, my vision blurring. My mouth fills with the metallic taste of blood, and I shake my head, trying to clear it. I can hear Kris behind me, yanking at the axe, trying desperately to free it from the tree. He must have come at me hard.

I crawl forward, my hands sinking into the snow, then push myself up to my feet. But Kris is already there, the axe raised high above his head. I kick out, my boot connecting with his stomach, and he grunts, stumbling back under the weight of the raised axe, then falling to his knees. The axe comes down, and I dive out of the way, landing hard on the frozen ground.

The axe sinks into the cold dirt inches away from me. Kris is out for blood. There's no question. Heart pounding, I roll onto my back. Kris is crawling towards me, trying to get to me. I kick him hard in the face. His head snaps back, and I scramble to my feet, my legs trembling beneath me. Kris recovers too quickly. His face twists with rage as he charges at me.

Desperation surges through me, and I do the only thing I can think of – I step towards him and punch him in the face. My fist connects with his nose in an explosion of pain. *Who knew punching someone in the face hurt so much?* But Kris stumbles back, clutching at his face, and I turn and run.

The sound of the axe slicing through the air behind me urges me forward, even as my body begs for rest. I don't know how much longer I can keep this up, but I know one thing for certain – If he wants me to stop, he's gonna have to kill me.

26

DETECTIVE DONNER

The Woods' home is a mix of flashing lights and urgent voices when I finally arrive. Police cars line the driveway, their red and blue strobes casting erratic shadows across the snow as I pull in and park. The air is thick with tension, the kind that makes every breath feel heavy.

The husband... *Barry is his name, right?* Is standing in the driveway, his face pale and drawn, clutching his son tightly against his chest. The boy's cries are muffled against his father's shoulder, his small body trembling with fear. Barry's eyes are wild, his voice rising as he yells at Officer Cane, who is trying to reassure the man.

I take a moment to assess the situation, then step out of my shop. Officer Wiseman heads towards me, expression grim. My head tilts up to look at him as he gets closer. The man is 6 feet 5 inches tall. "What's happening?" I ask, using my best "I'm in charge" voice.

Wiseman hesitates, his gaze flickering to the house before he speaks. "Pine and Thistle are dead. Psycho cut Pine's head off and shot Thistle in the back."

I absorb the information with a stoic nod, but inwardly I break a little. This is my fault. If only I'd caught this guy sooner. I prepare myself for more bad news. "The family?"

"Obviously, the husband and son are okay," Wiseman replies, indicating the husband and son standing in the driveway. "But the neighbor wasn't so lucky. Officers are taking his body down now. The killer hung him."

Fuck! Two dead officers and a dead neighbor? And that's on top of the eleven other victims. Forget retiring. I'm going to *be* retired for this shit show. My eyes shift to Barry, who is now in Cane's face, his voice rising in desperation. "Where's the wife?" I ask, dreading the answer.

Wiseman glances at Barry, then back at me. "Husband says his wife led the killer off into the woods behind their house and is insisting someone go after her."

I perk up. There's still hope. "Have you sent anyone?" I ask.

"Not yet. Working on it," Wiseman replies, his voice tinged with frustration.

I don't need to hear any more. I hurry toward Barry, my boots crunching in the snow. Irritably, I pull my coat hood up to keep the fluffy snowflakes falling from the sky from collecting in my hair. I hate when they melt, and my hair gets wet. *Does it eternally snow up here?*

Barry is trying to hand his son over to Cane, but Cane is resisting, his hands raised in a placating gesture. "Sir, you will have to wait for child services. I cannot take your son," Cane says, his voice firm but uneasy.

Barry's face twists with anger. "Then get out of the goddamn way, and I'll drop him off myself!" he shouts, his voice cracking under the strain.

I step in between the two men, redirecting Barry's angst towards me. "Mr. Woods. What seems to be the problem?"

Barry turns to me, his eyes desperate. Without warning, he grabs the front of my shirt, his grip surprisingly strong despite his injuries. "Please. Please! She's out there," he pleads, his voice breaking. He thrusts a tablet into my face, the screen glowing with a map. "She led him away from us, but someone has to go help her!"

Officers Cane and Shepherd exchange uneasy glances, their eyes flickering to me, waiting for my response. I try to keep my expression unreadable. *She's figured out how to lead us right to him. I'm impressed.* Although I'm not looking forward to a jaunt through the dark woods in this freezing weather, someone has to go, and it should be me.

"I'll go," I say.

Shepherd hesitates. "Sir, are you sure?"

"I'm sure," I reply, my tone leaving no room for argument.

Barry's grip on my shirt tightens. "I'll come with you."

I shake my head, my voice firm but gentle. "You need a hospital."

"I'm not abandoning her," Barry says, his voice trembling but resolute.

I place my hand on his shoulder, hoping it will help him focus on what I'm about to say. "This is not the time to abandon your son. I'll find her. I promise." I look over at Cane and use my best commander-in-chief tone. "Cane. Get this mess cleaned up and then come find me."

Cane nods, his concern palpable. "Yes, sir."

Barry hesitates, his eyes searching my face for reassurance. Finally, he hands over the tablet, his hands shaking. I take it, then turn and start up the icy driveway toward the backyard. The backyard is dark and full of way too much snow.

Why had she gone this way? It makes no sense.

The field stretches out before me, a vast expanse of white broken only by the dark shadows of trees. *How the hell am I going to follow this GPS through the woods?* I turn the tablet this way, then that, trying to get my bearings.

The moonlight glints off the snow, casting an eerie glow over the landscape. I finally get a handle on where I am versus where they are. They aren't close. My shoulders slump for a moment as I take in the daunting task ahead, then I begin trudging through the snow.

27
HOLLY

I'm barely running now. Clutching my side, my breath ragged, I limp along. I glance down at my stomach. I can feel the blood-soaked bandage under my coat. I press my hand harder against the wound, trying to encourage it to stop bleeding, but I'm pretty sure it ignores me.

Behind me, Kris is a stark splash of color against the snow, his Santa Suit visible in the moonlight. His movements are slow but relentless, his steps an uneven gate. He's dragging the axe now. I assume it's gotten heavy. It leaves a jagged trail in the powder beside him, and if I can see that, then he is too close.

I force myself to pick up the pace. The trees thin ahead, and I increase my speed another notch. *I could be close. Close to... somewhere... to someone... please anything!* For a moment, hope flickers in my chest.

I burst free from the woods, my lungs burning. I glance behind me, trying to gauge how immediate the danger is. It's too close. Kris is mere yards behind me and still coming. I turn back around only to skid to a halt at the edge of a wide river. Snow and gravel roll down the steep embankment as I stop mere inches from the ledge. I regain my balance and take a step back. Thankfully, the earth stops shifting underneath me.

Frantically, I search for a way across. The river is moving darkness down below, hard to see, but I can tell it's too wide and deep. I'd have to swim, and the last thing I need is hypothermia.

Think, Holly. Think.

My eyes dart around, searching for anything – a weapon, a hiding place, a miracle. And then I see it. A small shack, barely visible through the trees, its weathered wood blending into the shadows. A choked sob escapes my lips as I limp toward it, each step sending a fresh wave of pain through my body.

Kris breaks through the tree line next to me, his one good eye locks with mine, and he lets out a guttural growl, his pace quickening. I'm only halfway to the shack, equidistant from both Kris and shelter.

Kris sees the shack and realizes it's where I'm headed. He rushes at me, swinging the axe wildly. I duck, dropping down to my hands and knees as the blade swings over the top of me. I push myself up with a groan, then run for the open door of the shack. If I can just get inside. Suddenly, I'm hit from behind. The force of the blow sends me stumbling into the wall. I just manage to throw my hands up and catch myself before impact. Then rough hands are grabbing me by the shoulder and swinging me around. I'm brought face-to-face with my would-be killer. His eye is swollen shut, and blood drips down his face, but it doesn't seem to be slowing him down as much as I need it to. If anything, it makes him appear even more intimidating, like a walking nightmare.

Kris shoves the axe handle across my neck, and I push against it furiously. Kris puts all his weight behind it, and it's suddenly a contest of strength. A contest I will lose. The pressure on my throat threatens to crush my windpipe. I put all my strength into pushing against the handle on my neck. It's the only thing keeping me from being permanently silenced. I try to scream, try to muster the strength to push the axe off of me, but the scream comes out as a strained gurgle.

Stop focusing on this axe and do something, I tell myself.

I kick Kris in the leg. His foot slips on the snow, and Kris drops to one knee. The axe goes down with him. I turn back towards the shack, but I'm too close to open the door. *I thought I saw...* I peek around the side of the shack and look along the wall. *Yes!* I grab a large branch. It looks like a walking stick that someone has leaned against the side of the shack. I grab it and swing it all the way around. Thwack! It makes contact with Kris' stomach, and I hear the breath gush out of him in a whoosh. He doubles over, groaning, but I am not done. Bringing the stick back the other direction, I aim it at his head. Bam! It connects, and Kris's head flies to the side. His body follows, twisting in the air and then landing in the snow with a thud.

I don't wait to see if he's okay. I drop the large branch and run into the shack. I shut the door behind me, but it has a latch. The kind that requires a lock. I push open the door. Kris is already getting up. Frantically, I search the ground. *Come on. Come on!* Then I find it. A small but thick stick. I rush back into the shed, slamming the door shut. A loud THUD hits the door, startling me. I let out a small shriek, then realize it was just the axe being thrown at the door. I force the latch over the half-circle of metal, then push the stick through. It's a little too thick, and I have to force it. I grunt with the effort of pushing the too-large piece of wood through the small half-circle.

The door shudders as Kris hits it with his full weight, the wood groaning under the impact. The whole shack vibrates and seems to rock. Only the little stick, not yet through the half circle of metal, but sorta jammed into place, has kept the door shut at the unexpected impact.

I brace myself, my body pressed against the door, my feet slipping on the uneven floor, until I feel his weight lift off the door, then continue shoving the stick through the clasp. It tears off small chunks of itself as I force it through, then just as Kris throws himself against the door again, I've got it.

Kris throws himself against the door again and again. The impact is deafening, the entire shack shaking as if it might collapse. But the clasp holds... for now.

I slide to the floor, my legs giving out beneath me, my breath coming in shallow gasps. The pain in my side has become a constant, throbbing reminder of my mortality. I drop my head onto my knees and whimper. It feels so good to stop.

A memory, sharp and vivid, cuts through the haze of pain.

The sterile white of the hospital room is bathed in the soft glow of the late afternoon sun. Exhaustion clings to me like a heavy blanket, but it's a sweet exhaustion, the kind that comes after a long, arduous journey that ends in triumph. Barry sits beside me, his face alight with a joy so profound it seems to radiate from him. In his arms, swaddled in a soft blue blanket, lies Beau, his tiny face scrunched up in peaceful sleep.

I reach out my hand, trembling slightly, as I brush the back of one finger down Beau's impossibly soft cheek. A wave of love, so fierce and overwhelming that it brings tears to my eyes, washes over me. Barry's hand covers mine, his touch warm and reassuring. "He's perfect, Holly," he whispers, his voice thick with emotion. "So perfect."

In that moment, surrounded by the quiet miracle of new life, everything was perfect. The world outside the hospital room faded away, and there was only us, bound together by a love that felt both ancient and brand new. The long hours of labor, the excruciating pain, the fear that had gnawed at me for months – all of it vanished in the face of this tiny, perfect being.

Barry and I had spent countless hours preparing for his arrival, decorating the nursery, reading baby books, attending birthing classes. We had envisioned this moment, dreamed of holding our child in our arms, but the reality surpassed even our wildest dreams. The sheer, unadulterated joy, the overwhelming sense of responsibility, the profound connection that bound us together as a family – it was all so much more intense, so much more real than anything we could have imagined.

A montage of memories, both joyful and painful, flashes through my mind, a bittersweet tapestry of a life lived, a family forged, and a love tested.

Beau's first steps, Barry and I cheering him on, our faces beaming with pride. His first word, a garbled "Dadda" that sent shivers of delight down my spine. His first day of school. How he clung to me, peeking around my legs, eyes full of curiosity.

Christmases spent gathered around the tree, the air filled with laughter and the scent of pine needles. Summer vacations at the beach, the three of us building sandcastles, the sun warm on our skin. The quiet evenings spent reading bedtime stories, Barry's voice a soothing lullaby.

Barry and I fighting. The first night I slept in the guest room. Beau crying, begging us to stop yelling. The silence of a cold shoulder that never quite warmed up again.

The memories play through my mind like an old home video. *Is this the end then? Isn't that what happens? Your life flashes before your eyes.* But I don't feel like I'm dying. I feel.... Sad. Sad that we'd had so much and that we'd let it slip away, quietly, and without a fight, we'd let it go. We let anger and resentment build up between us and stopped being friends and lovers. A tear falls down my cheek, and I wipe it away. I have been so lonely for so long, and all along I have blamed Barry, but suddenly it seems so obvious... Barry has been there all this time. And he's been lonely too.

I think of Beau's face and never seeing it again. I think of Barry and leaving him like this, with all this unresolved hurt and anger between us, and I decide that that's not going to happen.

My whole body is trembling. I close my eyes and take a deep breath, then another, trying to steady myself.

Outside, Kris starts singing. "He knows where you are sleeping. He knows why you're awake..." Suddenly, the axe slams into the door of the shack. I scream unconsciously, no longer able to control my fight or flight instincts. The axe leaves a large slash in the door as he pulls it out. The shack is made of particle board. He'll be through it in no time.

"He sees that you've been bad, not good..."

My heart starts pounding, unnaturally strong in my chest. This shack is a temporary refuge, nothing more. I need a plan. I need a way to fight back. *But how?* I can't control my shivering. I feel frozen from the inside out. *Or am I in shock?* It's hard to know.

"Shoulda been good for your life's sake..." The axe slams into the wall I am leaning on, its shiny tip visible above me. I scream again and scramble away from it. I push myself to my feet, my legs wobbling, my side screaming, and scan the small space for anything I can use as a weapon. The small beams of moonlight shining through the holes in the roof don't reach the floor. It's entirely in shadow. I get down on my hands and knees and start to feel along the floor.

"Oh. You better look out, you don't want to die..." Kris continues his singing as the axe comes in through the other wall. The entire head of the axe easily breaking through the wood.

I move faster, frantically feeling along the edges of the floor." Ouch!" I jerk my hand back from whatever has poked my finger. Tentatively, I reach out into the dark and carefully find the sharp point of a nail. I grab it and lift it up. The weight of the board attached to it nearly pulls it out of my hands. I stare in disbelief, barely able to make out the edges of what I'm holding in the dark. In my hands, I hold a 2 x 4 with a long nail protruding from it. I almost smile, but it feels like smiling might be something I never do again. Instead, I grasp the bottom of the short board with both hands and swing it a couple of times to get a feel for it.

"Santa's here!" Kris hits the door again, the wood splintering around the edges. He's playing with me, enjoying having me trapped inside.

I back away from the door, my grip tightening on the 2x4. My hands are frozen, and holding onto the board is extremely painful. I hadn't grabbed gloves. I didn't want to wear them when I was climbing out the window, but now my hands are beyond numb. They scream in pain, but there is no way in hell I am putting this board down and putting them in my pockets.

I swing the 2x4 one more time. "Come on, Kris. Let's finish this."

28
KRIS

The axe comes down again and again, the latch rattling dangerously. I'm so close. So close to breaking through. *So close to getting mother.* My breath puffs in small clouds in front of my face, and it makes me laugh. I can see them out of my one good eye. I blow a few breaths and watch the clouds, smiling, then chide myself for being so childish. *Stupid. Stupid!*

Mother is being naughty. She's hiding. I giggle. *Maybe it's a game.* Hide and Seek. We'd loved hide-and-seek, mother and I. Mom used to pretend she couldn't find me, even though I was laughing out loud and she would have heard me. Still, she'd walked around saying, "Where could Kris be?" I smile thinking about it, then frown.

Why is she being so naughty? Doesn't she know I'm here to help? I'll do it nicely this time, without the blood. Did I forget to tell her? She has to come out of the little house so I can tell her.

"He knows that you've been bad, not good..."

I pause, tilting my head to listen. The shack is silent now, the only sound the faint rustle of the wind through the trees. But I can feel her inside, her fear, her pain... I'm drawn to it, love it, even though I don't want to. I can't resist it.

"Shoulda been good... for your life's sake."

I step back, narrowing my eye as I study the door. A couple more blows with my handy axe, and it will be chopped to bits. One strong blow, and I'll be inside. I decide to get a run at it, just for fun. I dance away from the shack, laughing, getting a good distance from the small structure. It's a shame to knock it down; it would make a good fort.

I raise the axe above my head. I can't stop smiling. So fun! *Running to kill mother. Running to knock her little house down.*

But then I stop. Something is wrong. I can feel... something watching me. Someone... *Dad?*

The air around me seems to shift, the silence growing heavier, more oppressive. A wind blows, and the trees make an eerie sound, their branches rattling in the breeze. I turn, my eyes scanning the clearing. The moonlight glinting off the snow casts long shadows that seem to stretch and twist.

Someone is out here, watching me. The feeling is like an itch under my skin where I can't scratch it. *I'm so close! Almost done!* I decide I don't care who they are. *I won't let them stop me.*

"Silent Night, Holy Night," I sing, hoping that it soothes Mother before the end.

29
HOLLY

Maniacal laughter rings through the silent night. Kris' laughter. It's coming from a ways away, but still in front of the door. He's gonna make a run at it. Fear grips me, low in my stomach. He's just been playing with me this whole time. He knows he can chop through the door or break the stick holding the door closed. My heart sinks as dread fills me. Hell, with one good hit, the entire shack could collapse... with me in it.

Kris's voice comes again, but it's farther away now. He's singing at the top of his lungs, his voice carrying through the night.

"Silent night, Holy night..."

My head snaps up, my brow furrowing. There's something else now—a new sound, faint at first but getting louder. Jingle bells. They're getting closer fast... The sound growing as if it's on a truck moving at top speed. My heart skips a beat. *What the hell is that?*

"All is calm..." Kris sings, unconcerned about the approaching bells.

Suddenly, the sound of hooves pounding against the snow fills the clearing. *Are those horses?* There's a loud thump, and I hear Kris cry out, his song cut off before he can finish his thought. The jingling bells are deafening as something heavy is dragged across the snow. As quick as they come, they begin to fade into the distance, both the hooves and the jingle bells.

I stand up on my tiptoes trying to see out the holes in the roof. The bells... *They're in the sky.*

What just happened? My mind races as I try to make sense of it. Then, just as the bells are almost indistinguishable, a voice — deep, booming, and unmistakably cheerful. "Merry Christmas to all, and to all a good night!"

My eyes scan the ceiling of the shack, willing the particle board to disappear and reveal the night sky so I can affirm that I'm not losing it. But the particle board stays put, and I can only see the moonlight shining through the small gaps in the roof as the jingle bells fade into the night, leaving behind an eerie stillness.

For a long moment, I just stand there, my heart pounding, my breath coming in shallow gasps. My mind is reeling, trying to process what just happened. *Was that... Santa? No. That's... crazy. But the jingle bells, the voice—it was real. Wasn't it?* For a moment, I worry that I've lost my mind.

I wait, but nothing happens. Slowly, I walk to the door and put one eye up to the crack between the door and the wall of the shed. I gasp and take a step back. Kris is lying mangled and unconscious in the snow. *I think Santa hit him with his sleigh.* I laugh hysterically. *Yep. I've lost it.*

But somehow, I know it's over. I sag in relief, my legs giving out underneath me. I lean against the wall as I slowly sink to the floor. A sob escapes my lips, then another and another. I drop my head into my hands, my knees pulled up protectively in front of me, and cry.

30
KRIS

A sudden noise distracts me- a faint jingling sound, like bells. It's soft at first, almost imperceptible, like bees buzzing in my brain, but it gets louder with each passing second.

I frown at the distraction, tightening my grip on the axe. *What is that?* I take a step forward, my eyes darting around the clearing. The sound is coming from the trees, or the... sky? But I don't see anything, just dark and impenetrable shadows. I decide to ignore it.

"All is calm..."

The jingling grows louder, more insistent, and then suddenly I can see it—a flash of movement, something big and dark, barreling towards me from the sky. It lands on the edge of the clearing, moving agilely through the trees. I feel my mouth fall open as my mind struggles to process the sight. *Is that... Santa?*

There isn't time to move, or even drop the axe I'm holding above my head, before I'm hit with the force of a freight train. It slams into me, and I fly through the air. *Finally! I've been waiting to fly all night.* The axe slips from my grasp, spinning away into the snow as I tumble through the air, then hit the hard-packed snow. And then I'm being trampled by small, hard feet. My mind goes numb. Maybe because I'm lying in the cold and wet snow.

The world spins around me, a blur of white and shadow, and then everything goes dark. The jingling bells fade into the distance. I watch them go. *Did you see that? Santa Claus!*

I lay there, my body twisted and broken, my mind struggling to make sense of what just happened. My breath comes in small, shallow gasps, each one more painful than the last. So much pain! *I have a job to finish.*

But the thought is faint and distant. I let my one good eye close and sigh as the cold seeps into my bones. A tear leaks out of my eye, and I feel it make its way down my temple and into my hair. *So alone. Always so alone.*

Suddenly, the biting cold of the snow recedes, replaced by a gentle, pervasive warmth. A soft light, a comforting, golden glow, and a voice...

"Kris...?"

It's her voice. *Mom?* It can't be. She's... she's gone!

But the voice persists, clearer now, closer. "Kris? Can you hear me?"

My eyes flutter open, or try to. The world is a hazy blur, but there she is. Mom. Younger than I remember, her face unlined, her eyes filled with a love that used to be my entire world. She's kneeling beside me, her hand reaching out, hovering just above my cheek.

"Mom?" The word is a whisper, a fragile thread of sound.

She smiles, a radiant, heartbreakingly beautiful smile. "Oh, my sweet boy. You're finally here. I've been waiting for you."

I try to sit up, to reach for her, but my body is leaden, unresponsive. The pain is still there, a dull throb beneath the surface of this... this vision? Dream?

"Where... where am I?" I manage to croak, my voice rough and unfamiliar.

She smiles. "It's Christmas Day. You're safe."

The warmth intensifies, becoming almost unbearably comforting. I can smell her... the faint scent of her perfume, the way her hair smelled just after she washed it.

"Mom!" The word bursts from my lips, and suddenly, I'm a child again. I'm small, safe, and enveloped in her love. I launch myself into her arms, burying my face in her neck. Unaware of the tears streaming down my face.

She holds me tight, her arms strong and sure. She hums, a lullaby I haven't heard in decades, a melody that speaks of safety and belonging.

"It's okay, my baby," she whispers, her voice soothing. "It's all over. We're together now. You're safe."

Together. The word resonates deep within me, striking a chord I thought long dead. This... this feeling. This is what I've been searching for. This is what was taken from me.

I pull back slightly, looking up at her face. "Dad...?"

Her eyes cloud over, looking sad for the first time. "He's not here, Kris."

For a moment, I feel sad, and then relieved. He can't hurt me anymore. And then I feel ashamed. Dad would be mad.

"It's okay," Mom says, stroking my hair. "He can't hurt you anymore." And I wonder if she can read my thoughts. Her hand brushes against my cheek, and the last vestiges of pain recede. The cold fades away, replaced by an all-encompassing peace. The fear, the rage, the twisted desires that have driven me for so long... they all dissolve, like snow melting in the spring sun.

I look at my mother, really look at her, for the first time as an adult. The kindness in her eyes, the strength in her gentle touch, the unwavering love that defined her.

"I... I tried, Mom," I whisper, the words catching in my throat. "I tried to be... good. To do what dad told me. I wanted us to be a family again."

She smiles, a knowing, forgiving smile. "I know you did, my sweet boy. I know."

"I hurt people," I confess, the shame and weight of my actions pressing down on me. "I was supposed to punish the naughty. I didn't want to do it, but Dad said I had to. Holly is on the naughty list, but I didn't punish her...I wanted to make it better...for you..."

Her hand tightens on mine, her gaze unwavering. "None of this is your fault. You were trying to find your way back to me, back to the light, back to when we were a family. That's all that matters now."

The light grows brighter, more intense. I can feel myself being drawn towards it, a gentle, irresistible pull.

"Am I... am I dying?" I ask, the question trembling on my lips.

Mother smiles down at me, her eyes shining with an otherworldly radiance. "Yes."

I sigh deeply and am vaguely aware of the cloud of white that escapes my body behind me for the last time.

For the first time in a long time, I don't feel any pain.

31
DETECTIVE DONNER

I wonder for the thousandth time why I've volunteered myself for this hellish job. This was what rookies were for, running through the woods at all hours of the night in the freezing cold. My lungs are burning, and my legs ache, but I push on. The radio squawks in my hand with both urgent messages and static, but I ignore it. I know why I've come. I have to find them. Kris and Holly. Their names echo in my mind, a desperate mantra. *Kris and Holly. Please let me find them in time.*

The snow is a treacherous blanket, hiding uneven ground and slick patches of ice. I stumble, right myself, and keep going. The tracks are faint, but they're there—two sets of footprints, one small and hurried, the other larger and heavier. Kris and Holly. I follow the tracks, my heart pounding against my ribs. The possibility of what I might find, urging me ever faster. *Please. Please!*

The trees thin ahead. I run down a slight incline, then slowly make my way up the small hill on the other side, panting like a dog in the heat. It's embarrassing. I obviously need to work out more. I see a small clearing ahead, even before I get to the top of the hill. A glint of silver shimmers in the weak morning sunlight, and I duck instinctively, but it's just a metal strip on the roof of what looks to be a small shack.

I bend down and use my hands to help push myself to the top of the hill, pretty much crawling up it. Yes, the snow and dirt shifting under my feet is making it more difficult, but *that's it*, I decide. *I am going to the gym this week.*

I finally crest the top of the ridiculously small hill and take a moment to breathe, bending over and putting my hands on my knees. In my defense, I have been running for a very long time through less-than-ideal conditions. I finally stand and take in the clearing, then do a double-take. Well, I've found them.

Holly stands just outside the shack, her back to me, her posture rigid. She's holding something in front of her, some kind of weapon by the way she's standing. *Is that a 2x4?* She doesn't seem to have heard my approach, even though I was less than subtle.

I slow my pace, my boots crunching softly on the snow. My head tilts to one side as I contemplate a dark stain at her feet. *Looks like blood. A lot of blood. A trail of blood.* And then I see him. Kris. His body is twisted and broken. I get a little closer, wanting to positively ID him, but his head... I force myself to look away. *Jesus!*

Of all the scenes I'd imagined while running through the woods, this was not one of them. For the life of me, I can't figure out what's happened here. Kris's body looks like it's been run over. There are even tracks leading away from him in the snow. But not tire tracks... *What kind of tracks are those,* I wonder, even as I notice that the tracks are red with Kris' blood.

My mouth falls open as I look around. I'm honestly not sure how to proceed. Holly is still standing there, frozen, like an intricate ice sculpture. The board must be heavy, but she holds it up in front of herself as if to say, "I will use this." Which is concerning because the only other person here, besides me, is dead.

I give her a wide berth, approaching slowly, my hands raised in a placating gesture. "Mrs. Woods?" I say, my voice gentle but firm. "Holly?" I notice as I circle around her that there is a long nail sticking out of the other side of the board. Definitely a weapon. "It's Detective Donner," I call. "Can you put the board down?"

She doesn't respond. Her eyes are fixed on Kris's body, her expression blank, almost vacant. Shock. It's a common enough reaction.

"Holly?" I say again, my voice is closer now.

She jumps, her body tensing, her grip on the board tightening. She raises it, the nail glinting in the dim light, but I'm still well out of reach.

"It's me," I say, my voice steady. "You're okay. Just put the board down."

She blinks, her eyes slowly focusing on me. I can see her cognitive mind trying to fight through the shock and fear to retake control. I give her all the time she needs. She's been through hell.

Finally, she looks down at the 2x4 in her hands. Her face twists into confusion and then revulsion. She throws it away, the board clattering to the ground, and takes a step back, wiping her trembling hands on her coat. *Her hands must be freezing.*

"He's dead," she says, her voice barely a whisper.

I nod, my eyes flicking to Kris's body. "I can see that," I say softly.

The weight of it all hits her then. She takes a step towards me, then another as her face crumbles. Her legs give out, and she collapses into my arms, sobbing uncontrollably.

I hold her, my arms wrapping around her in a firm but gentle embrace, and she buries her face in my shoulder.

"Thank God," she chokes out between sobs. "Thank God."

I hold her, my hand rubbing small circles on her back as she cries. My eyes are fixed on Kris's body. "You're safe," I tell her softly, over and over. So happy that it's true. So relieved that it's over. Of course, she'll probably never feel safe again. But that's a worry for another day.

32
HOLLY

The sky is just beginning to lighten, the first hints of dawn painting the horizon in soft hues of pink and gold. The air is crisp, biting at my skin, but I barely feel it. I'm standing just outside the shack, clutching something tightly in my hands. My fingers are numb, my knuckles white from gripping it so tightly.

Kris's body lies at my feet, twisted and mangled, his head crushed, blood pooling beneath him and staining the snow a deep, Christmas red. I can't look away. My mind is... numb. I don't feel anything. *He's dead, right? Actually dead.* I can't quite wrap my mind around it.

I know I should feel something... Guilt, or Relief, or... Happiness? But the only feeling I can name is 'tired.' I feel tired.

The sound of footsteps crunching through the snow pulls me from my trance. I look up, my heart skipping a beat, but it's not Kris. It's Detective Donner. My grip tightens reflexively. My knuckles ache, but I can't seem to let go. Detective Donner approaches me slowly, his hands raised in a placating gesture.

"Mrs. Woods?" he says, his voice gentle but firm. "Holly? It's Detective Donner. Can you put the board down?" He comes towards me like I'm a wild animal that might bite him or flee at any moment. Honestly, I feel like I could do either of those things. The urge to flee is almost irresistible.

"It's me. You're okay. Just put the board down," He says softly, and suddenly I feel... safe. My shoulders relax a bit.

Board? I think, then blink and blink again. My mind feels like it's underwater or struggling through a fog. *What board?*

The meaning of his words finally clicks into place, and I look down at my hands. I'm still holding the board with the nail sticking out of it, its tip glinting in the early morning light. I look at it like I've never seen it before. *This is what I've been holding onto so tightly?* I wonder as a wave of revulsion washes over me. I drop it, wanting it away from me. It clatters to the ground, and I take a step back, wiping my hands off on my coat. I still haven't said anything, I realize, so I say the most important thing I can think of.

"He's dead," I say, my voice barely above a whisper.

Donner nods, his eyes flicking to Kris's body. "I can see that," he says softly.

I'm safe. This man being here means I'm safe. I take a step towards him, then another as the weight of it all crashes down on me. My legs give out, and I collapse into Donner's arms, sobbing uncontrollably. He catches me, his arms wrapping around me in a firm but gentle embrace. I bury my face in his shoulder, my tears soaking into his coat.

"Thank God," I choke out between sobs. "Thank God."

Donner holds me, his hand rubbing small circles on my back as I cry. "You're safe," he tells me over and over, and I think that maybe, if he stands there and says it enough, maybe one day I'll believe him.

33
DETECTIVE DONNER

The crime scene is bustling with activity. Cops and paramedics move around the scene, careful not to disturb anything, their voices low and serious. Caution tape forms a perimeter around the area with Kris's body at the center, now covered with a tarp.

I stamp my feet, trying to introduce some circulation and resulting warmth into my toes. My legs ache, and more than anything, I want to sit down. I know I could go sit in the ambulance, in the front seat, or on the back, but I've chosen not to because I don't want to seem weak in front of my men. *I am too old for this.*

If what transpired here last night was more straightforward, I would have left already, but, as things are, I'm standing here freezing, my legs aching, while I wait for our forensics specialist to analyze the scene.

I glance over at the ambulance, wishing I were over there. This time for more than one reason. I don't want to hover, but I would love to be a fly on the wall. Cane is taking Holly's statement, and I am dying to know what she is telling him happened here. *Please let there be a simple explanation,* I beg the universe.

Holly is sitting on the edge of the ambulance, a blanket wrapped around her shoulders, her wounds bandaged, her hands still trembling. Cane says something, and she shakes her head, her eyes focused on the ground, not looking at him. Cane hesitates, then says, "Okay," loud enough for me to hear it. The way he says it makes it sound like he doesn't quite believe her and puts me even more on edge.

Finally, Cane walks away from her and approaches. I struggle to hide my impatience as he saunters up to me, a strange look on his face.

"What did she say?" I ask, my voice low and steady, despite my impatience.

Cane hesitates, a faint, infuriating smile tugging at the corners of his mouth. "She said Santa Claus did it, sir."

I look at him, my brow furrowing, not finding his statement in the least bit humorous. "She said Santa Claus did it?" The words sound ridiculous even to my own ears.

Cane chuckles, shaking his head like he's in on some cosmic joke. "Okay, not in those exact words. She says she was standing in the shack, holding the murder board, as Kris hacked at the shack with his axe. He's singing and having a great old time, when suddenly she hears jingle bells."

"Jingle bells," I repeat, my tone flat, the absurdity of it all starting to grind on my nerves.

"Mm-hmm," Cane says, nodding, his amusement growing. "Coming from the sky, in that direction." He points a gloved finger towards the trees, his expression still ridiculously entertained. "Then she says there was a commotion, like a small herd of animals running by, along with the sound of something large sliding over the snow. Then she says the jingle bells get farther away, and she hears someone wish her a Merry Christmas—again from the sky, but this time from that direction." He points in the opposite direction, his smile widening into a full-blown grin. "Eventually, she comes out of the shack and finds him exactly like this." He gestures with a sweep of his arm toward the tarp-covered lump that used to be Kris.

I think, my jaw tightening. Cane is beaming at me, clearly enjoying the hell out of this. "That's her official statement, sir. She was in the shack the whole time. Didn't see a thing."

"Perfect," I mutter, rubbing a hand over my face, the rough stubble scratching against my palm. I sigh, the weariness finally winning, my shoulders slumping under the weight of this whole damn mess. "Well, she obviously didn't kill him with the..." I trail off, my gaze flicking towards Cane.

"Murder board?" Cane offers, his smile widening even further, at the cute little nickname he's given her weapon.

I give him a look that could curdle milk. "No, sir," Cane says quickly, though his idiotic smile doesn't even flicker. "Looks to me like he got on Santa's naughty list."

"Cane?" I say, my voice sharp, the last vestiges of my patience wearing thin.

"Yes, sir?" He chirps, still grinning like an idiot.

"Will you please shut up?"

Cane's smile gets even bigger, and I can't help but smile on the inside. "Yes, sir." He quips happily, as I shake my head and walk away.

Resigned, I walk towards the crime scene and our forensic tech, Mary.

She's crouched near the edge of the caution tape, her gloved hands gently brushing snow away from something on the ground.

"Tell me something, Mary," I say, my voice weary. "What have we got?"

Mary stands, brushing snow off her neatly pleated slacks. "Well, Detective, it appears as if he was murdered by Santa Claus."

I give her a flat stare. "Come on, Mary. Be serious."

"Unfortunately, I am," she says, her tone utterly matter-of-fact. She walks a few steps within the taped-off area and gestures to the snow-covered ground. "Hoof tracks start here. There are none before it, and none beyond the tape, but right here... reindeer tracks."

"Reindeer tracks?" I repeat, my voice tinged with utter disbelief.

"Mm-hmm," Mary says, nodding. "Very specific reindeer tracks. The kind that only live in the northern regions of the planet."

"Like the North Pole?" I guess, my tone exasperated.

"I mean, I can't say for certain until we've properly analyzed them, but if I had to guess, I would say yes."

I rub a hand over my face, exhaling sharply. "Go on."

Mary walks a few more steps and points to the ground again. "The hoof prints all go in the same direction and are lined up, exactly like they would be if the animals were harnessed. The tracks are accompanied by two runner tracks—the kind that would be made by a very large, very heavy sleigh."

I frown, my arms crossing tighter over my chest. "Mary, isn't it possible that a sleigh could have gone through here before these two showed up, and the tracks were simply erased before and after this particular spot?"

Mary shakes her head. "The tracks are fresh, Detective. The snow has just been churned up. You can see it." She walks over to Kris's body and crouches beside the tarp. "And if you look at our victim here, all of his wounds are consistent with the witness's statement."

I walk over to see what she's showing me, my expression grim. Mary pulls back a corner of the tarp, revealing Kris's mangled arm. "Here's where she said she stabbed him—the wound is consistent with a small pocketknife." She moves to his legs. "And here's where she says she shot him. But it's hard to see his other wounds because he's clearly been trampled to death by... reindeer."

"Stop saying that," I say, my voice sharp.

Mary looks up at me, her expression apologetic. "I'm sorry, Detective, but these are very clearly reindeer tracks. And you can see here,"—she points to Kris's exposed head—"that one of the runners on the sleigh ran right over his head, crushing his skull. These dark pieces in the snow are bits of blood and brain matter. I'll collect what I can, but..."

I stare at her, my jaw tightening. "So, you're telling me Santa Claus came down from the sky, ran over this guy, flew off with his magic fucking reindeer, and then wished Holly Woods a Merry Christmas?"

Mary shrugs. "Well, I can't say that it was definitely Santa Claus, and I know nothing about him wishing her a Merry Christmas, but magic reindeer seems consistent with the evidence here... Not that I'd put that in my report."

I just stare at her, my expression a mix of disbelief and utter frustration. Mary gives me a small, apologetic smile before walking away, her footsteps crunching on the snow-covered ground as she goes to get more evidence bags. She's a good forensic pathologist, sharp, dedicated, and usually unflappable. If she's talking about magic reindeer, then this particular crime scene has her stumped.

I glance back at Kris, sprawled on the ground, his body twisted at an unnatural angle, most of him showing out from under the tarp, exactly how Mary left him. The festive Santa suit is torn and bloodied, the once white trim stained a gruesome crimson. An axe lies a few feet away from him, its blade untarnished and glinting in the sunlight. *Where did that come from? An Axe? He'd never used an axe before...* Holly must have really done a number on him. The thought makes me smile.

I do a slight backbend to ease the pressure on my lower back, then glance again at the dead body on the ground, and this time something miraculous happens. For the first time in what feels like months, the crushing weight on my chest begins to lift. It's like the pressure of a relentless storm has finally broken, and a fragile ray of sunlight is peeking through the clouds. *He's dead.* And while we can't explain exactly how that happened, at least it's finally over.

This whole damn case has been a nightmare. A goddamn, twisted, gruesome nightmare. I've been living in a horror movie, and I was starting to think there would be no escape. My shoulders droop in exhaustion. I haven't slept properly in weeks. The faces of the victims have haunted my dreams, while the relentless need to catch this guy... I glance at him again, lying there crushed and silent, and realize I never did. Never did catch him. But it doesn't matter. It's over.

The weight of responsibility lifts. He's gone, and I can rest, can sleep now. And when the faces of the dead visit me in my dreams, I can tell them that we got him... sort of... That someone got him, and that he didn't win. He never got his last victim. I look over at Holly just to make sure she is actually sitting there. She looks bad. We should have taken her to a hospital already, but I don't move. Instead, I stand there breathing easily for the first time in weeks.

The endless dead ends, the taunting clues, the bizarre MO, the sheer, senseless violence of it all... It's finally over. For the first time in a long time, I don't have to worry that someone out there is going to be murdered. *At least not in my precinct, thank God!*

My phone rings, startling me, and I pull it out of my pocket. My fingers are clumsy from a mixture of fatigue and relief. I check the caller ID. It's my wife. I've forgotten to call her, and I obviously didn't make it home last night. She's gonna be pissed, but I don't care. I answer, excited to talk to her for the first time in days. Failure is hard on a relationship, I realize with a twinge of guilt. I've been practically avoiding her, not wanting her to see me as the inept Detective who couldn't catch a killer. But she didn't deserve that. She, of course, has just wanted to be there for me. Help me. But then, what could she have done?

"Hi," I say, and I can't keep the giddy relief out of my voice. "I'm so sorry I didn't call. Everything is okay." I say before she can speak.

Her voice, warm and familiar, fills my ear. "You're okay? Is... everyone... okay?" She doesn't want to ask if another woman has been murdered. My shoulders slump a little, but I decide to suck it up and tell her the whole truth. I've had a win, but not without losses. "Officers Thistle and Pine were murdered last night, along with a neighbor." I hear her gasp on the other end of the line, and I give her a moment before continuing, "But his intended victim evaded him, and he's dead."

There's a long pause on the other end of the line while she takes that in.

"It's over," I say softly. "It's finally over." I let the words sink in, savoring the taste of them. *Over*. It's a beautiful word.

It suddenly occurs to me that Elizabeth, my wife, has just spent Christmas Eve alone, waiting for me to come home, unaware of what was happening. A pang of sorrow and regret shoots through me. I've been unkind. I clear my throat, *ahem*. "I'm sorry I didn't call sooner, and that I've been so..." I don't want to finish that thought, so instead I say. "I love you, Elizabeth."

"I love you, too," she says, and I can hear the smile in her voice. She deserved an apology. I'm glad I finally gave her one. "Merry Christmas," she says, and her forgiveness feels like another Christmas present. The first one being the dead body on the ground. I suppose that was my gift from Santa this year. I groan at my own humor.

Okay, time to get back to work. "Honey, I'll be home in a couple of hours. I just have to make sure everyone is doing their job here, but I'll hurry. Okay?"

She says, "Okay," and we hang up.

Mary starts loading Kris into a body bag with the help of Wiseman and Shepherd. *Good. Time to get the hell out of here.* I look for Holly and find her hugging her son with Barry standing close beside them. *Where did they come from?* I decide to give her a moment, but talking to her one last time is on my list.

34
HOLLY

My hands tremble as I tug the blanket closer around me. I can't get warm. My toes have frozen solid inside my boots, and every icy breeze wafts right through my thin pajamas. My coat and the blanket the EMT gave me offer some protection from the crisp early morning air, but it feels like I'll never be truly warm ever again.

My eyes stray to the dead body mere feet from where I'm sitting. They keep doing that. I reassure myself that he's still there, still dead. *He's gone.* I tell myself again. *He's dead.* I need my mind to accept this fact so that my body can relax. I still feel on high alert.

And then I hear it—a voice calling my name.

"Mom!"

My heart leaps in my chest, and I turn, my breath catching. Barry and Beau are running toward me. Their faces are pale, but they move easily, and I offer a silent *thank you* to the universe that they are okay.

"Beau!" I cry, my voice breaking. I stumble to my feet, the blanket falling to the ground as I run toward them.

Beau's small hand is clutching Barry's, his eyes wide as he takes in the scene. Barry's arm is bandaged, his face drawn, but his eyes lock onto mine, and I see relief there and maybe even love.

The snow slows me down as I hurry towards them, each step a struggle, but I don't care. I am so damn relieved to see them.

Beau lets go of his father's hand and runs even faster. We collide, my arms wrapping around him, pulling him tightly against me. He feels so small, so fragile, and I start to cry. I can't help it, can't stop the tears. "Are you okay?" I choke out, my voice shaky. I push him back to arm's length, frantically checking him over, but he seems fine. No cuts, no bruises. Just scared. I pull him back into a tight hug, my body shaking with sobs. *What is wrong with me?* But no matter what I do, I can't stop the tears.

Barry reaches us, and I stand, throwing my arms around him. He holds me tightly, his grip firm but gentle, and I bury my face in his shoulder. "I'm so sorry," I whisper, my voice breaking. "I'm so sorry."

"You have nothing to be sorry about," Barry says, his voice steady but soft. He pulls back slightly, his hands cupping my face, and I can see in his eyes that the past is behind us. The anger and resentment, the past hurts and blame—they're over. He wraps me in his arms, and for the first time since I discovered the Kris Kringle Killer in my car, I relax. *Safe. I'm finally safe.*

Barry and I separate, and I turn to Beau. He's staring at Kris's body as officers lay a body bag on the snow next to him. I crouch down beside my son, my hands resting on his shoulders, and point his body toward Kris's mangled body. Normally, I wouldn't allow him to see something so gruesome, but this time is different. He needs to know, to see, to be sure.

"Do you see that?" I ask.

Beau nods, his eyes wide and scared.

"He's dead," I say, my voice steady. "And you never have to be afraid of him again. He's gone, forever. Santa Claus killed him."

Beau's eyes grow even wider. "Santa Claus?" he asks, his voice small.

"Yes," I say, nodding. "He came down with his sleigh and saved me."

"He really did?" Beau whispers, his voice filled with awe.

"He really did," I say, smiling through my tears. "And if anyone ever asks if you believe in Santa Claus, you can say yes. And you can tell them your mother believes in him, too."

I pull Beau into another hug, holding him tightly. When I stand, I take Barry's hand in one of mine and Beau's in the other. The three of us are about to leave when Detective Donner calls out from behind us.

"Mrs. Woods. A moment, please."

We stop, and I turn to face him. This man came after me. He didn't save me, but he feels like my savior nonetheless. "Detective?" I say respectfully.

"I just need one more moment of your time," he says, his tone polite but firm.

I nod, letting go of Barry and Beau's hands. "Go ahead," I say softly. "I'll be right there."

Barry hesitates, his eyes searching mine, but then he nods, taking Beau's hand and leading him away. I turn back to Donner, my arms crossing over my chest. "Yes, Detective?" I ask.

"So, it's your official report that Santa Claus killed this man?" he asks, his tone neutral but his eyes sharp.

I take a deep breath. There's no way he thinks I did this, so I'm not alarmed by the question, but I choose my words carefully, just as I did for the report, sticking to the facts and not making any wild claims. "I told Officer Cane what happened," I say carefully. "I didn't actually see..."

Donner cuts me off. "And you've never met Kris Conners before tonight?"

"Never," I say, my voice firm.

"And you can't think of any reason why he might have been targeting you?" he asks, his eyes narrowing slightly.

I look at him for a long moment, my jaw tightening. "No," I say, my voice final. "I cannot."

We stare at each other, the silence stretching between us. Finally, Donner relents, nodding. "Well... if you remember anything that might actually help us, please let me know. Enjoy the rest of your holiday."

"You too, Detective," I say, my voice steady.

He nods and walks away, leaving me standing there. I turn to follow Barry and Beau, but my phone rings. I pull it out of my pocket, my stomach dropping when I see the caller ID. *Sugarplum.*

I consider ignoring it, but then I answer. He speaks immediately, his voice warm and familiar.

"There you are! Merry Christmas. Can you talk? Or is your husband..."

Guilt washes over me at what I'm about to do. My voice sounds flat and unemotional as I say, "It's over."

"What?" he says, his voice filled with confusion.

"We're done," I say, my tone final.

"Holly..." he starts, his voice pleading and confused.

"Never call me again," I say, and then I hang up, my hands trembling. *I've hurt so many people.* I take a deep breath, pushing down the anger and guilt, and look up to see Barry and Beau walking back toward me. I am taking this secret to the grave. No one will ever know that it was my fault... *All my fault.* He'd been right all along, my Kris Kringle Killer.

"Who was that?" Barry asks, his brow furrowed.

"Wrong number," I say, forcing a smile.

"Can we leave?" Barry asks, his arm slipping around my shoulders.

"Yes," I say, nodding. "Let's go home."

Barry hesitates, his expression wary. "By home, you mean a hotel, right? Because we are never going back to that house."

"Agreed," I say, my voice firm.

The house needs to be burned down. Too many people have died there... they're ghosts, restless and sad. I shiver as the image of Rudy hanging from our balcony floats across my mind, followed by the memory of the officer's head rolling off his body and landing at my feet. I can still hear the sound it made when it hit the ground.

Barry's arm tightens around me, and I smile at him gratefully, then take Beau's hand. The three of us start walking, the snow crunching beneath our feet. The sun is warm on my face, and for the first time in what feels like forever, I feel confident that it's all going to work out, that we are always going to be a family. I guess we have Kris Conners to thank for that.

SHARE THE HOLIDAY HORROR!

Thank you for taking a ride into the twisted winter world of this story.

I hope the journey thrilled you, chilled you, and kept you flipping pages long past bedtime.

If *Slay Ride* made you smile, scream, or sleep with the lights on,

please leave a quick review.

Your words make a difference. Your review helps other readers discover this book and keeps indie storytelling alive.

Plus, it's nice! Don't make Santa put you on his naughty list. If you had fun, tell the next reader why.

Wishing you a Merry, jolly, and only slightly unhinged Christmas season!

— **Olivia Dunkley**

EPILOGUE
NICHOLAS CONNERS

I read the headline again.

Kris Kringle Killer Killed in Sleigh Accident

I haven't paid much attention, but wasn't this Kris Kringle killer, my Kris? My son? Were they saying he was dead? I continue reading. ...*the killer, who terrorized the city with a string of gruesome murders, was killed during a confrontation with one of his intended victims, Holly Woods... bizarre circumstances... appears to have been trampled to death by reindeer pulling a sleigh... People on the street are claiming that Santa Claus, unhappy about being impersonated by a serial killer, took matters into his own hands... The investigation is still underway...Holly and her family have given their statements...*

My teeth clench. He's dead? My son! My only legacy. I focus again on the article. *Holly Woods*. This bitch has robbed me of the only thing I had left. My son! Not that he was much of a legacy, the crazy lunatic. The one time I'd called him at the asylum, he'd kept telling me that he didn't want to be Santa Claus anymore. Whatever that meant.

Sniveling brat had loved his mother too much. What kind of pussy falls apart because his mother dies?

Of course, now that he'd dressed up as Santa Claus and gone on a killing spree, killing women who were having affairs, it made a little more sense. A feeling akin to pride flows through me as I think about it. Who would have thought? I would have never guessed he'd have the nerve. It almost made me proud. *The bitches. They'd all gotten what they deserved. Had they no decency, no loyalty? The whores! They should have been faithful, loyal to the hand that fed and cared for them.*

I hadn't called Kris again after that. I hadn't seen the point.

Nevertheless, I'd had plans for him. He was my progeny, and I still had assets on the outside, money and accounts. I'd had big plans. There were only 2 short years left on my sentence. After a lifetime of being in here, I'd planned to go collect my son and turn him into a man fitting of the Conners' name. Instead, he was dead because of this Holly bitch.

I focus on her picture in the paper. There are two images, one of her looking pretty beat up, with blood spattered across her face, and her hair wild and disheveled. The other: a family photo of the three of them, dressed impeccably and smiling. The perfect happy family. I look into the smiling face of her young son. How interesting that she thinks she can kill my son but keep hers. A small, humorless smile tilts up the corners of my lips as a beautiful thought floats across my mind.

I'll kill her son in front of her, so she understands how it feels, before I strangle her with my bare hands. I would finish what my son started. The idea feels like the beginning of something new. A new life purpose. Now that Kris was gone, there was nothing, nothing for me on the outside. No one waiting, no one to find... only

Holly Woods. And when she was lying dead and cold, all would be right again.

You've Read the Book, Now Watch the Movie!

Now Streaming on:

TubiTV
Amazon Video
AppleTV
Roku Channel
Fandango
Xumo Play
Plex
Hoopla

Printed in Dunstable, United Kingdom